James Thomson

The works of James Thomson

With his last corrections and improvements. Vol. 4

James Thomson

The works of James Thomson
With his last corrections and improvements. Vol. 4

ISBN/EAN: 9783337113308

Printed in Europe, USA, Canada, Australia, Japan

Cover: Foto ©Andreas Hilbeck / pixelio.de

More available books at **www.hansebooks.com**

THE

WORKS

OF

JAMES THOMSON.

VOL. IV.

THE
WORKS
OF
JAMES THOMSON.

VOLUME THE FOURTH.

CONTAINING,

EDWARD and ELEONORA,

TANCRED and SIGISMUNDA,

AND

CORIOLANUS.

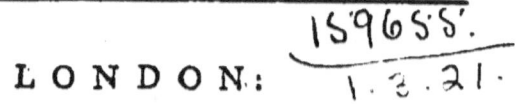

LONDON:

Printed for W. Bowyer, W. Strahan, J. Rivington,
B. Law, W. Owen, R. Horsfield, T. Longman,
T. Caslon, S. Crowder, G. Keasley, D. Wilson
& Co. T. Cadell, T. Lowndes, T. Davies, Rich-
ardson & Richardson, and H. Baldwin.
MDCCLXXIII.

G. V. Neijſ ſc.

Edward and Eleonora.

EDWARD and ELEONORA.

A

T R A G E D Y.

TO HER

ROYAL HIGHNESS

THE

Princefs of *Wales.*

MADAM,

IF I take the liberty, once more, to crave the protection of your ROYAL HIGHNESS, for another Tragedy of my writing, it is becaufe I am led, almoft unavoidably, to it, by my fubject. In the character of ELEONORA I have endeavoured to reprefent, however faintly, a

B 2 PRIN-

PRINCESS diftinguifhed for all the virtues that render greatnefs amiable. I have aimed, particularly, to do juftice to her inviolable affection and generous tendernefs for a PRINCE, who was the darling of a great and free people.

Their defcendants, even now, will own, with pleafure, how properly this addrefs is made to your ROYAL HIGHNESS. I am, with the profoundeft refpect,

MADAM,

Your ROYAL HIGHNESS'S

Moft humble, and

moft devoted Servant,

PROLOGUE.

By a FRIEND.

IN former Times, when fierce religious rage,
And priestly sway deform'd each suffering age,
All manly wit, all useful learning lay
In darkness lost, nor hop'd returning day.
Religion then was stain'd by cruel deeds.
And free-born Reason stoop'd to craft and creeds.
But happier we!—And tho' to-night we show
What fatal ills from blind devotion flow,
'Tis not that we such rage renew'd can fear,
Or dread the hand of persecution here—
Our scene would wide humanity impart;
Would breathe extensive candour thro' the heart;
Show true religion even to error kind,
And claim the perfect freedom of the mind.
If too the poet paints a noble strife
'Twixt the fond husband and the generous wife;
If all the father in his *voice complains,*
And all the mother in her *tender strains;*

If

If these best passions prompt the pleasing woe,
Indulge it freely———Nature bids it flow :
Where parent Nature leads, you cannot stray ;
And what she wills, 'tis virtue to obey.

    Fond of BRITANNIA's *fame, and just to* YOU,
He bids old English honour *live anew,*
And calls your great first EDWARD *up to view.*
But if his line too weak, his stroke too faint,
The graceful figure, in full light, to paint ;
In candid part his honest meaning take,
And spare the poet for the hero's sake.

EPILOGUE.

EPILOGUE.

By a FRIEND.

THESE Poets are such fools !—The man behind,
Who wrote this play—a simple soul, I find—
Believes with all his heart, there was a wife,
Who needs would die—to save a husband's life !
He in the printed chronicles has read it :
And true it is—Sir Richard Baker said it.

Why what an ass these books do make a man ?
Read nature—then believe it—you who can.
Look round this town—the question is not—whether
Spouse dies for spouse : but who will live together ?
Of old, they say, a husband was a lover :
But, thank our stars ! those foolish days are over :
To such substantial prudence are we come,
We wed not heart to heart—but plumb to plumb.
What sense ? what beauty ? are not now the things :
But can he settle—up to what she brings ?

Yet in this easy, all-forgiving age,
Bear with such moral fooleries—on the stage.
Perhaps too, there may be some gentle soul,
Who rather likes to weep—than win a vole ;
Who thinks that there are charms in generous love,
And would to Edward Eleonora prove.

The

The Persons represented.

EDWARD, Prince of *England*,	Mr. *Delane*.
EARL of *Glofter*,	Mr. *Rofco*.
THEALD, Archdeacon of *Liege*,	Mr. *Roberts*.
SELIM, Sultan of *Jaffa*,	Mr. *Ryan*.
ELEONORA, Princefs of *England*,	Mrs. *Horton*.
DARAXA, an *Arabian* Princefs,	Mrs. *Hallam*.

Affaffin, Officers, &c.

SCENE, EDWARD's *tent in the camp before* Jaffa, *a city on the coaft of* Paleftine.

Edward and *Eleonora.*

A

T R A G E D Y.

ACT I. SCENE I.

Prince EDWARD, THEALD *Archdeacon of* Liege, *Earl of* GLOSTER.

EDWARD.

I Will no longer doubt. 'Tis plain, my friends,
That with our little band of *English* troops,
By all allies all western powers deserted,
All but the noble knights that guard this land,
The flower of *Europe* and of christian valour,
Nought can be done, nought worthy of our cause,

Worthy

Worthy of *England*'s heir, and of the name
Of *Lion-hearted* RICHARD ; whofe renown,
After almoft a century elaps'd,
Shakes through its wide extent this caftern world.
What elfe could bend the *Saracen* to peace,
Who might, with better policy, refufe
To grant it us ? yes, to the prince of *Jaffa*
I will accord the peace he has demanded :
And tho' my troops, impatient, wait the fignal
To ftorm yon walls, yet will I not expofe,
In vain attempts, valour that fhould be fav'd
For better days, and for the public welfare.
Rafh fruitlefs war, from wanton glory wag'd,
Is only fplendid murder—What fays *Theald ?*
Approves my reverend father of my purpofe ?

THEALD.

Edward, illuftrious heir of *England*'s crown,
I muft indeed be blinded with the zeal
Of this our holy caufe, to think your arms,
Thus all-forfaken, thus betray'd, fufficient
To reach the grandeur of your firft defign.
And, from the yoke of infidels, to free
The facred city, objeft of our vows ;
Yet this, methinks, this *Jaffa* might be feiz'd :
That ftill were fomething, an aufpicious omen
Of future conqueft—But, unfkill'd in war,
To you, my lord, and *Glofter*'s wife experience,
I this fubmit.

EDWARD.

EDWARD.

Speak, *Gloster*, your advice,
Before I fix my lateſt reſolution.

GLOSTER.

You know, my lord, I never was a friend
To this cruſado. My unchang'd advice
Is ſtrenuous ſtill for peace. Nor this, I urge,
From our deſerted arms, and cauſe betray'd,
But from the ſtate of our unhappy country.
Behold her, *Edward*, with a filial eye,
And ſay, is this a time for theſe adventures?
Behold her then with deep commotion ſhook,
Beneath a falſe deluſive face of quiet:
Behold her bleeding yet from civil war,
Exhauſted, ſunk; drain'd by ten thouſand arts
Of lawleſs impoſition, prieſtly fraud,
Italian leeches, and inſatiate *Rome*;
That never rag'd before with ſuch groſs inſult,
With ſuch abandon'd avarice. Beſides,
Who knows what evil counſellors, again,
Are gather'd round the throne! In times like theſe,
Diſturb'd, and lowring with unſettled freedom,
One ſtep to lawleſs power, one bold attempt
Renew'd, the leaſt infringement of our charters,
Would in the giddy nation raiſe a tempeſt.
Return, my prince. You have already ſav'd
Your father from his foes, from haughty *Leiſter*:
Now ſave him from his miniſters, from thoſe
Who hold him captive in the worſt of chains—

EDWARD,

EDWARD.

You, *Gloster*, fav'd us both.

GLOSTER.

I did my duty;
Even while I join'd with *Leister*, did my duty—
I hope I did—He, who contends for freedom,
Can ne'er be juftly deem'd his fovereign's foe:
No, 'tis the wretch that tempts him to fubvert it,
The foothing flave, the traitor in the bofom,
Who beft deferves that name; he is a worm
That eats out all the happinefs of kingdoms.

Edward, return; lofe not a day, an hour,
Before this city. Tho' your caufe be holy,
Believe me, 'tis a much more pious office,
To fave your father's old and broken years,
His mild and eafy temper, from the fnares
Of low corrupt infinuating traitors:
A nobler office far! on the firm bafe
Of well-proportion'd liberty, to build
The common quiet, happinefs and glory,
Of king and people, *England*'s rifing grandeur.
To you, my prince, this tafk, of right, belongs.
Has not the royal heir a jufter claim
To fhare his father's inmoft heart and counfels,
Than aliens to his int'reft, thofe, who make
A property, a market of his honour?

One reafon more allow me to fuggeft
For peace, immediate peace—fhould blind misfortune,
In this far diftant hoftile land, opprefs us;

A chance

A chance to which our weaknefs ftands expos'd :
What, *Edward*, of thy princefs would become,
Thy *Eleonora* ; fhe, whofe tender love
Thro' ftormy feas, and in fierce camps attends thee ?
What of thy blooming offspring? charg'd with thefe,
To give our courage fcope were cruel rafhnefs.

EDWARD.

Enough, my lord, I ftand refolv'd on peace ;
And will to *England* ftrait.—But where, alas,
Where fhall we cover our inglorious heads ;
When gay with hope the people round us prefs
To hear by what exploits we have fuftain'd
The fame of *Richard*, and of *Englifh* valour ?
Shall I, my generous country, I be rank'd
With thofe weak princes, who confume thy wealth,
And fink thy name in idle expeditions ?
Perfidious *France !* Be this the ruling point
Of my whole life and paffion of my foul,
To humble thee, proud nation!—Meantime, *Glofter*,
See that the captive princefs be reftor'd,
Daraxa, to the fultan of this city,
Whofe bride fhe is—We wage not war with women.

SCENE

SCENE II.

EDWARD, THEALD, GLOSTER, *an* Officer *belonging to the Prince.*

OFFICER.

One from the prince of *Jaffa,* Sir, demands
Your secret ear on some important message.

EDWARD.

Conduct him to my tent——   [Officer *goes out.*
           He brings, I judge,
The sultan's last instructions for this peace.
Here wait : I may your faithful counsel want.

SCENE III.

THEALD, GLOSTER.

THEALD.

Whatever woes, of late, have clouded *England*;
Yet must I, *Gloster,* call that nation happy,
On whose horizon smiles a dawning prince
Of *Edward*'s worth and virtues.

GLOSTER.

             True, my friend;
Edward has great, has amiable virtues,
That virtue chiefly which befits a prince :

                  He

He loves the people he muſt one day rule;
With fondneſs loves them, with a noble pride;
Eſteems their good, eſteems their glory his.
One inſtance it becomes me to recount,
That ſhows the genuine greatneſs of his ſoul.
Tho' I have met him in the bloody field,
He fighting for his father, I for freedom;
Yet bears his boſom no remaining grudge
Of thoſe diſtracted times: to me his heart
Is greatly reconcil'd—Virtue! beyond
The little unforgiving ſoul of tyrants!

 Now will I tell thee, *Theald*, whence I ſtoop
To wear the gaudy chains of court-attendance,
At theſe grey years; that ſhould in calm retirement
Paſs the ſoft evening of a buſtling life,
And plume my parting ſoul for better worlds.
Amidſt his many virtues, youthful *Edward*
Is lofty, warm, and abſolute of temper:
I therefore ſeek to moderate his heat,
To guide his fiery virtues, that, miſled
By dazzling power and flattering ſycophants,
Might finiſh what his father's weaker meaſures
Have try'd in vain. And hence I here attend him,
In expeditions which I ne'er approv'd,
In holy wars—your pardon, reverend father—
I muſt declare I think ſuch wars the fruit
Of idle-courage or miſtaken zeal,
Sometimes of rapine and religious rage,

To

To every mifchief prompt.

THEALD.

You wrong, my lord,
You wrong them much.   To fet this matter only
Upon a civil footing : fay, what right
Had robbers rufhing from *Arabian* defarts,
Fierce as the funs that kindled up their rage,
Thus, in a barbarous torrent, to bear down
All *Afia*, *Afric*, and profane their altars ?
And to repel brute force by force is juft.
Nay, does not even our duty, int'reft, glory,
The common honour of the chriftian name,
Require us to reprefs their wild ambition,
That labours weftward ftill, and threatens *Europe?*

GLOSTER.

Yes, when they burft their limits, let us check them :
And with a firmer hand than thofe loofe chriftians,
The moft corrupt and abject of mankind,
Slaves, doubly flaves, who fuffer'd thefe *Arabians*,
In virtue their fuperiors as in valour,
Without refiftance to o'er-run the world.
By rage and zeal, 'tis true, their empire rofe :
But now fome fettled ages of poffeffion
Create a right, than which, I fear, few nations
Can fhew a better.   Sure I am 'tis madnefs,
Inhuman madnefs, thus, from half the world,
To drain its blood and treafure, to neglect
Each art of peace, each care of government ;

And

And all for what? By spreading desolation,
Rapine and slaughter o'er the other half,
To gain a conquest we can never hold.
   I venerate this land. Those sacred hills,
Those vales, those cities, trod by saints and prophets,
By GOD himself, the scenes of heavenly wonders,
Inspire me with a certain awful joy.
But the same GOD, my friend, pervades, sustains,
Surrounds and fills this universal frame;
And every land where spreads his vital presence,
His all-enlivening breath, to me is holy.
   Excuse me, *Theald*, if I go too far:
I meant alone to say, I think these wars
A kind of persecution. And when that,
That most absurd and cruel of all vices,
Is once begun, where shall it find an end?
Each in his turn, or has or claims a right
To wield its dagger, to return its furies;
And, first or last, they fall upon ourselves.

        EDWARD, *behind the Scenes.*

Inhuman villain! is thy message murder?

        THEALD.

Ha! heard you not the prince exclaiming murder?

        GLOSTER.

Should this barbarian messenger—
              [*Moving towards the noise.*
         'Tis so!

                 SCENE.

S C E N E IV.

THEALD, GLOSTER; *to them prince* EDWARD
wounded in the arm, and dragging in the assassin.

EDWARD.

Detested wretch! And does the prince of *Jaffa*
Send base assassins to transact his treaties?
There—take thy answer, ruffian!
  [*Stabs him with the dagger he had wrested from him.*
                              Blow too hasty!
I should have sav'd thee for a fitter death.

ASSASSIN.

I would have triumph'd, christian, in thy rage.
For know, thou vile destroyer of the faithful!
That tho' my erring dagger miss'd thy heart,
Yet has it fir'd thy veins with mortal poison,
Whose very touch is death—ALLAH be prais'd!
O glorious fate! Prophet, receive my soul! [*Dies.*

EDWARD, *after a short pause.*

Why gaze you with amazement on each other?
Are we not men, to whom the various chances
Of life are known?

GLOSTER.

                  Ha! poison! did he say?
Then is at once my prince and country lost!
O fatal wound to *England!*

THEALD.

      Quick, my lord,
Retire and have it dreſt, without delay;
Ere the fell poiſon can diffuſe its rage,
And deeply taint your blood.

EDWARD.

        The princeſs comes!
O ſave me from her tenderneſs!

SCENE V.

EDWARD, THEALD, GLOSTER; *to them the
princeſs* ELEONORA.

ELEONORA.

      My *Edward!*
Support me!—Oh!

EDWARD.

      She faints—My *Eleonra!*
Look up, and bleſs me with thy gentle eyes!—
The colour comes, her cheeks reſume their beauty,
And all her charms revive-- Hence, ſpurn that carcaſs;
A ſight too ſhocking for my *Eleonora.*

ELEONORA.

And lives my *Edward,* lives my deareſt lord,
From this aſſaſſin ſav'd—Alas! you bleed!

EDWARD.

EDWARD.

'Tis nought, my lovely princefs!—A flight wound—

ELEONORA.

But, ah! methought, I entering heard of poifon,
Tainting the blood—What! was the dagger poi-
fon'd?—
Ha! filent all? will none relieve my fears?—

GLOSTER.

Madam, reftrain your tendernefs a moment—
The prince delays too long—Let him retire.
Meanwhile, the troubled camp fhall be my care;
Left the bafe foe fhould make a fudden fally,
While yet our troops are ftunn'd with this difafter;

EDWARD.

I thank thee, noble *Glofter*.   Nor, alone
Support my troops; go, roufe them to revenge;
Tell them their injur'd prince will try their love,
Their valour foon—And you, my friend, good *Theald*,
Attend the princefs—Chear thee, *Eleonora!*
I cannot, will not, leave thee long, to vex
Thy tender foul with aggravated fears.

THEALD.

Behold *Daraxa*, the falfe fultan's bride.

SCENE

SCENE VI.

Eleonora, Theald, Daraxa.

DARAXA.

Princess of *England*, let me share thy grief.
Whence flow these tears ? and what this wild alarm,
This noise of murder and affassination ?

ELEONORA.

Alas ! the prince is wounded by a ruffian ;
And with a poison'd dagger, as I fear.
Yet none will ease me of this racking thought—
Nay, tell me, *Theald,* since to know the worst
Is oft a kind of miserable comfort ;
What has befal'n the prince ? For this slight wound
Could never thus o'ercast the brave with terror.

THEALD.

I dare not, princess, dally with your fate.
An impious villain, from the sultan *Selim,*
Pretended to the prince a secret message,
About the peace in treaty.   Dreading nought,
He left us here, and to his tent retir'd,
There to receive this execrable envoy.
Strait with the prince alone, the fierce affassin
Attempted on his life ; but, in his arm,
He took, it seems, the blow, and from the villain
Wresting the dagger, plung'd it to his heart.

This

This laſt we ſaw, aud heard the inhuman bigot,
Who deem'd himſelf a martyr in their cauſe,
Boaſt, as he dy'd, the prince's wound was poiſon'd—

ELEONORA.

Then all I fear'd is true! then am I wretched,
Beyond even hope!

DARAXA.

    A villain from the ſultan!—

ELEONORA.

Ah the diſtracting thought! And is my life!
My love! my *Edward!* on the brink of fate!
Of fate that may this moment ſnatch him from me!

DARAXA.

What! *Selim* ſend aſſaſſins? and beneath
A name ſo ſacred? *Selim*, whoſe renown
Is incenſe breathing o'er the ſweeten'd eaſt;
For each humane, each generous virtue fam'd;
Selim! the rock of faith! and ſun of honour!

ELEONORA.

O complicated woe! The chriſtian cauſe
Has now no more a patron, and reſtorer;
England no more a prince, in whom ſhe plac'd
Her glory, her delight, her only hope;
Theſe deſolated troops no more a chief;
No more a huſband, a protector, I,
A friend, a lover! and my helpleſs children
No more a father!

DARAXA.

    Pardon, gentle princeſs,

If in this whirlwind of revolving paffions,
That fnatch my foul by turns, i have forgot
To pay the tribute which I owe thy forrows—
But I myfelf, alas! am more unhappy!

ELEONORA.

What woes can equal mine? who lofe, thus vilely,
The beft! the braveft! lovelieft of mankind!—

DARAXA.

You only *lofe* the man you love, but I,
O infupportable! muft learn to *hate*,
To *fcorn* what once was all my pride and tranfport!
Should *Edward* die by this accurfed crime,
(Which Heaven forbid) he dies admir'd, belov'd,
In the full bloom of fame and fpotlefs honour.
To you, the daughter of illuftrious grief,
Your tears remain, and fadly-fweet refleftion;
You with his image, with his virtues, ftill,
Amidft the penfive gloom, may converfe hold:
While I—Ah! nothing meets my blafted fight
But a black view of infamy and horror!
What is the lofs of life to lofs of virtue!—
And yet how can this heavenly fpark be loft?
No! virtue burns with an immortal flame.
He is bely'd—fome villain has abus'd him.

THEALD.

I honour, Madam, this your virtuous grief:
But that the fultan did employ th' affaffin
Is paft all doubt—Behold the falfe inftruftions,

By

By which he gain'd admittance.

[Giving her the letter the prince had dropt.

DARAXA.

Ha!—'Tis fo!
His hand! his feal!—From my detefting heart,
I tear him thus for ever!—Perifh, *Selim!*
Perifh the feeble wretch, who more bewails him!
That were to fhare his guilt!—Unhappy princefs!
Now let me turn my foul to thy affiftance—
There is a cure, 'tis true——

ELEONORA.

A cure, *Daraxa?*
O fay, what cure?

DARAXA.

No; it avails not, Madam;
None can be found to rifque it.

ELEONORA.

None to rifque it?
Quick tell me what it is, my dear *Daraxa.*

DARAXA.

To find fome perfon, that, with friendly lip,
May draw the poifon forth; at leaft, its rage
And mortal fpirit. This will bring the wound
Within the power of art: but certain death
Attends the generous deed.

ELEONORA, *kneeling.*

Then hear me, Heaven!
Prime fource of love! Ye faints and angels, hear me!
I here devote me for the beft of men,

6

Of

Of princes and of hufbands. On this crofs
I feal the cordial vow: confirm it Heaven!
And grant me courage in the hour of trial!

THEALD.

O tendernefs unequal'd!

DARAXA.

Gloriôus princefs!

ELEONORA.

Go, *Theald*, quickly find the earl of *Glofter*,
And with him break this matter to the prince.
As for the perfon, leave that tafk to me.
I with *Daraxa* will your call attend;
O all ye powers of love, your influencè lend.

The End of the Firft Act.

ACT II. SCENE I.

GLOSTER, THEALD.

GLOSTER.

NO, *Theald*, no ; he never will confent—
  I know him well; he ne'er will purchafe life,
At fuch a rate : befides, in aid of love,
His generous pride would come, and deem it bafenefs.

THEALD.

Then is yon fun his laft.   The blackning wound
Begins already to confefs the poifon——
Meantime, my lord, both friendfhip and our duty
Demand, at leaft, the trial.   Well I know,
That, poife his life with hers, he would as nothing
Efteem his own : but fure the life of thoufands,
The mingled caufe at once of heaven and earth,
Should o'er the beft the deareft life prevail.

GLOSTER.

Alas ! my friend, you *reafon*, *Edward loves*.
How weak the head contending with the heart !
Yet be the trial made—Behold he comes.

SCENE II.

EDWARD, GLOSTER, THEALD.

EDWARD, *entering.*

O thou bright fun ! now haft'ning to those climes,
That parent-isle, which I no more shall see ;
And for whose welfare oft my youthful heart
Has vainly form'd so many a fond defign ;
O thither bear, resplendent orb of day,
To that dear spot of earth, my last farewel !

And oh ! eternal Providence, whose course,
Amidst the various maze of life, is fix'd
By boundless wifdom, and by boundless love,
I follow thee, with resignation, hope,
With confidence and joy ; for thou art good,
And of thy rifing goodness is no end !

Well met, my dearest friends !—It was too true,
The villain's threatning, and I nearly touch
That awful hour which every man must prove,
Yet every man still shifts at distance from him.
Come then, and let us fill the space between
Thefe last important moments, whence we take
Our lateft tincture for eternity,
With folemn converse and exalting friendship—
Nay—*Theald*—*Glofter*—wound me not with tears
With tears that fail o'er venerable cheeks !

What could the princefs more?—Ah! there, indeed,
At every thought of her, I feel a weight,
A dreadful weight of tendernefs, that fhakes
My firmeft refolution—Where is fhe?

THEALD.

She burns with fond impatience to attend you.

EDWARD.

And how, brave *Glofter*; did you leave the camp?

GLOSTER.

The camp, Sir, is fecure: each foldier there
From indignation draws new force and fpirit.
O 'tis a glorious, an affecting fight!
Thofe furrow'd cheeks that never knew before
The dew of tears, now in a copious fhower
Are bath'd. Around your tent they, anxious, crowd,
Rank over rank: fome prefling for a look;
Some fadly mufing, with dejected eye;
Some, on their knees, preferring vows to heaven;
And, with extended arm, fome breathing vengeance.
" Bafe *Saracens*, they cry, perfidious cowards!
" But blood fhall wafh out blood—Ah! poor atone-
        ment,
" Did the whole bleeding city fall a victim!"

EDWARD.

Alas, that to repay their faithful love
I cannot live!—Yet moderate their zeal;
And let the fword of juftice only ftrike
The faithlefs *Selim*, and his guilty council.
My new-departed fpirit, juft efcap'd
From the low fev'rifh paflions of this life,

Would

Would grieve to fee the blood of innocence
With that of guilt confounded, ſtain my tomb.

THEALD.

Permit me, Sir, the hopè, that you yourſelf——
I ſpeak it on juſt cauſe—may live to puniſh
This breach of all the ſacred rights of men.

EDWARD.

Why will you turn my thoughts, from earth enlarg'd,
To ſoft enfeebling views of life again?

THEALD.

Not to a vain deſire of life, my lord,
I would recal them; but inſpire each hope,
Adviſe each poſſibility to ſave it.
And there is yet a remedy.

EDWARD.   -
        Deluſion!

THEALD.

The fair *Arabian* princeſs mention'd one.

EDWARD.

She one!—*Daraxa!*—ſomething to complete
Her lover's crime.

THEALD.

      You could not wrong her thus,
Had you beheld the tempeſt of her ſoul,
Her grief, her rage, confuſion, when ſhe heard
Of *Selim*'s baſeneſs; had you ſeen that honour,
That glorious fire which darted from her eyes;
'Till in a flood of virtuous ſorrow ſunk
She almoſt equal'd *Eleonora*'s tears.

C 3   EDWARD.

EDWARD.

What was it she propos'd ?

THEALD.

It was, my lord,
To find some person, who, with friendly lip,
Might draw the deadly spirit——

EDWARD.

I have heard
Of such a cure ; but is it not, good *Theald*,
An action fatal to the kind performer ?

THEALD.

Yes, surely fatal.

EDWARD.

Name it then no more.
I should despise the paltry life it purchas'd.
Besides, what mortal can dispose so rashly
Of his own life ? Talk not of low condition,
And of my public rank : when life or death
Becomes the question, all distinctions vanish ;
Then the first monarch and the lowest slave
On the same level stand, in this the sons
Of equal Nature all.

THEALD.

Allow me, Sir,
If 'tis a certain, an establish'd duty,
Than duty more, the height of human virtue,
To sacrifice a transitory life.

For

For that kind fource from whence it is deriv'd,
And all its guarded joys, our dearest country;
It may be justly facrific'd for those
On whom depends the welfare of the public.
And there is one, my lord, who stands devoted,
By folemn and irrevocable vows,
To die for you.

EDWARD.

To die for me!—Kind Nature!
Thanks to thy forming hand, I can myself,
Chearful, fustain to pay this debt I owe thee,
Without the borrow'd fufferings of another.
No, *Theald*, urge this argument no more.
I love not life to that degree, to purchafe,
By the fure death of fome brave guiltlefs friend,
A few uncertain days, that often rife,
Like this, ferene and gay, when, with fwift wing,
A moment wraps them in difaftrous fate.

GLOSTER.

Did we confult to fave your fingle life,
Was that the prefent queftion, thy refufal
Were juft, were generous. But, my lord, this perfon,
Who ftands for you devoted, fhould, in that,
Be deem'd devoted for the chriftian caufe,
The common caufe of *Europe* and thy country;
Dies for the brave companions of thy fortune,
Who weeping now around thy tent conjure thee
To live for them, and *England*'s promis'd glory.
O fave our country, *Edward!* fave a nation,

The

The chosen land, the last retreat of freedom,
Amidst a world enslav'd!—Cast back thy view,
And trace from farthest times her old renown.
Think of the blood that, to maintain her rights,
And guard her sheltering laws, has flow'd in battle,
Or on the patriot's scaffold.   Think what cares,
What vigilance, what toils, what bright contention,
In councils, camps, and well-disputed senates,
It cost our generous ancestors, to raise
A matchless plan of freedom : whence we shine,
Even in the jealous eye of hostile nations,
The happiest of mankind.—Then see all this,
This virtue, wisdom, toil and blood of ages,
Feh'd it ready to be lost for ever.

In this important, this decisive hour,
On thee, and thee alone, our weeping country
Turns her distressful eye ; to thee she calls,
And with a helpless parent's piercing voice.
Wilt thou not live for her ? for her subdue
A graceful pride, I own, but still a pride,
That more becomes thy courage and thy youth
Than birth and public station ? Nay, for her,
Say, wouldst thou not resign the dearest passions ?

EDWARD.

O, there is nothing, which for thee, my country,
I, in my proper person, could not suffer !
But thus to sculk behind another's life,
'Tis what I have not courage to support,
It makes a kind of coward of me, *Gloster.*

But

But let me fee this friend, whofe generous virtue
Fxceeds what even my favourable thoughts
Had imag'd in the felfifh race of man.
The purpofe claims the merit of the deed ;
And ere I die I muft requite his friendfhip.
Conduct him hither, *Theald.*

SCENE III.

EDWARD, GLOSTER.

EDWARD.

Ah, my *Glofter,*
You have not touch'd on fomething that here pleads
For longer life, beyond the force of reafon,
Perhaps too powerful pleads—my *Eleonora?*
To thee, my friend, I will not be afham'd
Even to avow my love in all its fondnefs.
For oh there fhines in this my dearer felf!
This partner of my foul ! fuch a mild light:
Of carelefs charms, of unaffected beauty,
Such more than beauty, fuch endearing goodnefs,
That when I meet her eye, where cordial faith,
And every gentle virtue mix their luftre,
I feel a tranfport that partakes of anguifh !
How fhall I then behold her, on the point.
To leave her, *Glofter,* in a diftant land ?

C 5.

For

For ever in a ſtormy world to leave her ?
There is no miſery to be fear'd like that
Which from our greateſt happineſs proceeds!

S C E N E IV.

EDWARD, GLOSTER, THEALD *preſenting the
princeſs* ELEONORA *as the perſon he went to
bring,* DARAXA.

EDWARD.

O Heaven !—what do I ſee ?—I am betray'd !—

                      [*Turning away,*

ELEONORA.

Edward !

EDWARD.

O, 'tis too much ! O ſpare me, Nature !

ELEONORA.

Not look upon me, *Edward?*

EDWARD.

Eleonora !

How on this dreadful errand canſt thou come ?

ELEONORA.

Behold me kneel——

EDWARD.

Why kneel you, beſt of women !
You ne'er offended, ne'er in thought offended !
Thou art all truth, and love, and angel-goodneſs !

     ι   W hy

Why do you kneel? O rise, my *Eleonora!*

ELEONORA.

Let me fulfil my vow.

EDWARD.

O never! never!

ELEONORA.

Let me preserve a life, in which is wrapt
The life of thousands, dearer than my own!
Live thou, and let me die for thee, my *Edward!*

EDWARD.

For me!—thy words are daggers to my soul.
And wouldst thou have me then thus meanly save
A despicable life? a life expos'd
To that worst torment, to my own contempt!
A life still haunted by the cruel image,
Of thy last pangs, thy agonizing throws,
The dire convulsions of these tender limbs;
And all for one—O infamy!—for one,
By love, by duty bound, each manly tie,
Even by a peasant's honour to protect thee?
Yet this, tho' strong, invincible, is nought
To what my wounded tenderness could urge
Against thy dire request—But should Fate demand
The life we love, then, then, we must exert
The greatest act of human resignation,
We must submit. But wouldst thou have me, say,
Doom thee myself? with voluntary choice,
Nay, by a barbarous crime, untimely snatch
This worst of ills? Would *Eleonora* make me

Of

Of all mankind the most completely wretched?

ELEONORA.

Plead not the voice of honour. Well I know,
There is no danger, pain, no form of death,
Thou wouldst not meet with transport to protect me.
But I, alas! an unimportant woman,
Whose only boast and merit is to love thee;
Ah, what am I, with nameless numbers weigh'd?
With myriads yet unborn? All ranks, all ages,
All arts, all virtues, all a state comprizes?
These have a higher claim to thy protection.
Live then for them.—O make a generous effort!
What none but heroes can, bid the soft passions
The private stoop to those that grasp the public.
Live to possess the pleasure of a God,
To bless a people trusted to thy care.
Live to fulfil thy long career of glory,
But just begun. To die for thee be mine.
I ne'er can find a brighter, happier fate:
And fate will come at last, inglorious fate!
O grudge me not a portion of thy fame!
As join'd in love, O raise me to thy glory!

EDWARD.

In vain is all thy eloquence. The more
Thou wouldst persuade, I with encreasing horror,
Fly from thy purpose.

ELEONORA.
Dost thou love me, *Edward?*

EDWARD,

EDWARD.

Oh!—If I love thee ?—Witnefs heaven and earth!.
Angels of death that hover round me, witnefs!
Witnefs thefe blinded eyes, thefe trembling arms,
This heart that beats unutterable fondnefs,.
To what an agony I love thee ——

ELEONORA.

Then-

Thou fure wilt fave me from the worſt of pains.

EDWARD.

O that I could from all engrofs thy fufferings !
Pain felt for thee were pleafure !

ELEONORA.

Hear me, *Edward*.

I fpeak the ſtrictest truth, no flight of paffion,
I fpeak my naked heart.—To die, I own,
Is a dread paffage, terrible to Nature,
Chiefly to thofe who have, like me, been happy.—
But to furvive thee—O, 'tis greatly worfe !
'Tis a continual death ! I cannot bear
The very thought— O leave me not behind thee !

EDWARD.

Since nought can alter my determin'd breaft,
Why doft thou pierce me with this killing image ?

ELEONORA.

Ah ! felfifh that thou art ! with thee the toil,
The tedious toil of life will foon be o'er ;
Thou foon wilt hide thee in the quiet grave :
While I, a lonely widow, with my orphans,

Am

Am left defencelefs to a troubled world,
A falfe, ungrateful, and injurious world !——
Oh ! if thou lov'ft me, *Edward*, I conjure thee;,
By that celeftial flame which blends our fouls !
By all a father, all a mother feels !
By every holy tendernefs, I charge thee !
Live to protect the pledges of our love,.
Our children !—

EDWARD.

Oh !——

ELEONORA..

Our young, our helplefs——

EDWARD..

Ch !—

Diftraction !—Let me go !

ELEONORA.

Nay, drag me with thee——
To the kind tomb—Thou canft not leave our children !.
Expos'd, by being thine, beyond the loweft !
Surrounded with the perils of a throne !—

EDWARD.

Cruel ! no more embitter thus our laft,
Our parting moments ! Set no more the terrors
Of thefe beft paffions in array againft me !
For by that Power, I fwear, Father of life !·
Whofe univerfal love embraces all
That breathes this ample air ; whofe perfect wifdom
Brings light from darknefs, and from evil good ;

To

To whom I recommend thee, and my children:
By him I fwear! I never will fubmit
To what thy horrid tendernefs propofes!'

GLOSTER.

My lord——

EDWARD.

Oh!—thefe emotions are too much—
I feel a heavy langnor fteal upon me:
The working poifon clogs the fprings of life.
Conduct me to my couch—Ah! *Eleonora!*
If we ne'er meet again—This one embrace—
Yet fink not to defpair—Heaven may preferve me
By means fuperior to all human hope.

ELEONORA.

I will not, cannot quit thee!——

SCENE V.

ELEONORA, DARAXA.

DARAXA.

Princefs, ftay.
Think not the hand of death is yet upon him,
Refiftlefs fleep will firft opprefs his fenfes,
Before the laft convulfive pangs come on;
For fo the numming poifon oft begins
To fpread its dark malignity.——

ELEONORA.

ELEONORA.

Ha!—Sleep?—

Then is the time—Thanks to infpiring Heaven!
But come, and ere the venom fink too deep,
Swift let me feize the favouring hour of fleep..

The End of the Second Act.

ACT III. SCENE I.

GLOSTER.

O Miracle of love! O wond'rous princefs!
'Tis fuch as thou, who keep the gentle flame,
That animates fociety, alive,
Who make the dwellings of mankind delightful.
What is vain life? an idle flight of days,
A ftill-delufive round of fickly joys,
A fcene, of little cares and trifling paffions,
If not ennobled by fuch deeds of virtue?
And yet this matchlefs virtue! what avails it?
Th' afflicting angel has forfook the prince,
And now pours out his terrors on the princefs.
Forfook him, faid I?—No; he muft awake
To keener evils than the body knows,
Which minds alone, and generous minds can feel.
O Virtue! Virtue! as thy joys excel,
So are thy woes tranfcendent; the grofs world
Knows not the blifs or mifery of either—
    The prince forfakes his couch—He feems renew'd
In health—Ah, fhort deceitful gleam of eafe!

SCENE

SCENE II.

EDWARD, GLOSTER.

EDWARD, *advancing from his couch.*

Hail to the fresher earth and brighter day!
I feel me lighten'd of the mortal load
That lay upon my spirits.   This kind sleep
Has shed a balmy quiet thro' my veins.
Whence this amazing change?————
   But be my first chief care, Author of good!
To bend my soul in gratitude to thee!
Thou, when blind mortals wander thro' the deeps
Of comfortless despair, with timely hand,
Invisible, and by unthought-of ways,
Thus lead'st them forth into thy light again.

GLOSTER.

How fares my lord, the prince?

EDWARD.

            To health restor'd,
Only a kind of lassitude remains,
A not unpleasing weakness hangs upon me:
Like the soft trembling of the settled deep,
After a storm.

GLOSTER.

Father of health be prais'd!

EDWARD.

· EDWARD.

The moment that I funk upon my couch,
A fick and troubled flumber fell upon me;
Chaos of gloomy unconnected thought!
That, in black eddy whirl'd, made fleep more dreadful
Than the worft waking pang.   While thus I tofs'd,
Ready to bid farewel to fuffering clay,
Methought an angel came and touch'd my wound.
At this the parting gloom clear'd up apace;
My flumbers foften'd; and, with health, return'd
Serenity of mind, and order'd thought,
And fair ideas gladdening all the foul.
Aerial mufic too, by fancy heard,
Sooth'd my late pangs and harmoniz'd my breaft.
Thro' fhades of blifs I walk'd, where heavenly forms
Sung to their lutes my *Eleonora's* love—
But where is fhe? the glory of her fex!
O dearer, juftly dearer, far than ever!
Quick, let me find her, pour into her bofom
My full full foul, with tendernefs o'ercharg'd,
With glad furprife, with gratitude and wonder.—
    Ha! why this filence? this dejected look?
You caft a drooping eye upon the ground.
Where is the princefs?

GLOSTER.

　　She, my lord, repofes.

EDWARD.

Repofes!—No!—It is not likely, *Glofter*,

　　　　　　　　That

That she would yield her weeping eyes to sleep,
While I lay there in agonies--away!
I am too feeble then to know the truth.
Say, is she well?

GLOSTER.

Now show thy courage, *Edward*—

EDWARD.

O all my fears! I shall start out to madness!
What!—while I slept?

GLOSTER.

Yes——

EDWARD.

Misery! distraction!
My peace, my honour is betray'd for ever!
O love! O shame! O murder'd *Eleonora!*

S C E N E III.

GLOSTER.

Unhappy prince! go find thy *Eleonora*,
And in heart-easing grief exhale thy passion:
All other comfort, now, were to talk down
The winds and raging seas.—But yonder comes
Th' *Arabian* princess. From her tears I learn
The moving scene within.

SCENE

SCENE IV.

GLOSTER, DARAXA, *a Meſſenger from* SELIM,
attending at ſome diſtance.

DARAXA.
O! 'tis too much!

I can no more ſupport it.
GLOSTER.
Generous mourner,

How is it with the princeſs *Eleonora?*
DARAXA.

Struck by the poiſon on her couch ſhe lies,
A roſe ſoft-drooping in *Sabzan* vales,
Beneath the fiery dog-ſtar's noxious rage.
O chriſtian chief. I never ſhall forget
The ſcene theſe melting eyes have juſt beheld,
With mingled tears of tenderneſs and wonder.
GLOSTER.

How was it, Madam?
DARAXA.

When this pride of women,
This beſt of wives, which in his radiant courſe
The ſun beholds. when firſt ſhe, ſickening, felt
Th' imperious ſummons of approaching fate,
All rob'd in ſpotleſs white ſhe ſought the altar;
And, proſtrate there, for her departing ſoul,

The

The prince her hufband, and her orphan-children,
Implor'd th' Eternal Mind.—As yet fhe held
Her fwelling tears, and in her bofom kept
Her fighs reprefs'd : nor did the near approach
Of the pale king of terrors dim her beauty ;
No, rather adding to her charms, it breath'd
A certain mournful fweetnefs thro' her features.
But as th' increafing bane more defperate grew,
Wild to her bed fhe rufh'd, and then, indeed,
The lovely fountains of her eyes were open'd,
Then flow'd her tears.—"Connubial bed, fhe cry'd,
" Chafte witnefs of my tendernefs for him,
" To fave whofe life I unrepining die
" In bloom of youth, farewel!—Thou fhalt, perhaps,
" Receive a fairer, a more happy bride ;
" But never a more faithful, never one
" Who loves her hufband with a fonder paffion."
Here flow'd her tears afrefh ; with burning lip
She prefs'd the humid couch, and wept again.
At laft, while weary forrow paus'd, fhe rofe,
And, fearing left immediate death might feize her,
Demanded to be led to fee the prince ;
But fear of chafing from his eyes, too foon,
The falutary fleep that heal'd his pangs,
Reftrain'd her trembling footfteps. On her couch,
Abandon'd to defpair, fhe funk anew,
And for her children call'd. Her children came.
A while, fupported on her arm, fhe ey'd them,
With tears purfuing tears a-down her cheek, .

With

With all the fpeechlefs mifery of woe—
J fee her ftill—O God !—the powerful image
Diffolves me into tears !

GLOSTER.

Madam, proceed.
Such tears are virtue, and excel the joys
Of wanton pride.

DARAXA.

Then, ftarting up, fhe went
To fnatch them to a mother's laft embrace ;
When'ftrait reflecting that the piercing poifon
Might taint their tender years, fhe fudden fhrunk
With horror back—" O wretched *Eleonora !*
" (She weeping cry'd) and muft I then not tafte
" The poor remaining comfort of the dying,
" To fee a hufband, clafp my deareft children,
" And mix my parting foul with theirs I love ?"
Her fad attendants, that till then had mourn'd
In filent forrow all, at This, gave way
To loud laments—She rais'd her languid eye,
And cafting on them round a gracious fmile,
To each by name fhe call'd, even to the loweft,
To each extended mild her friendly hand,
Gave, and, by turns, receiv'd a laft farewel.
Such is the dreadful fcene from which I come.

GLOSTER.

How heighten'd now with *Edward*'s mingled woes !
Why are my lingering years referv'd for this ?

DARAXA.

DARAXA.

Come nearer, you, the meſſenger of *Selim*,
And bear him back this anſwer—His chief aim,
He ſays, in ſtooping to ſolicit peace,
Was from the chains of infidels to ſave me.
What! was it then to reſcue me he ſent,
Beneath an all-rever'd and ſacred name,
Beneath the ſhelter of his hand and ſeal,
A murdering wretch, a ſacrilegious bigot,
To ſtab at once the gallant prince of *England*,
And public faith? nay, with a poiſon'd dagger
(Such his inhuman cowardice) to ſtab him?
So well, 'tis true, he judg'd; the chriſtian prince
Had now been mingled with the harmleſs dead;
If his bright princeſs, glorious *Eleonora*,
Had not redeem'd his dearer life with hers.
You heard in what extremity ſhe lies.
Go, tell the tyrant then—O heaven and earth!
O vanity of virtue! that *Daraxa*
Should e'er to *Selim* ſend ſo fell a meſſage——
I will ſuppreſs its bitterneſs—Yet tell him,
This crime has plac'd eternal bars between us.
See my laſt tear to love——*Arabian* wilds
Shall bury 'midſt their rocks the loſt *Daraxa*.
Away!

GLOSTER.

　　Behold, they bear this way the princeſs,
Once more to taſte the ſweetneſs of the ſun,
Ere yet to mortal light ſhe bid farewel.

SCENE

SCENE V.

GLOSTER, DARAXA, THEALD, EDWARD,
ELEONORA *borne in by her Attendants on a
couch.*

ELEONORA, *entering.*

A little on, a little further on,
Bear me, my friends, into the cooling air.
O chearful fun! O vital light of day!

EDWARD.

That fun is witnefs of our matchlefs woes,
Is witnefs of our innocence——Alas!
What have we done to merit this difafter?

ELEONORA.

O earth! O genial roofs! O the dear coaft
Of *Albion*'s ifle! which I no more fhall fee!——

EDWARD.

Nay, yield not to thy weaknefs, *Eleonora!*
Suftain thyfelf a little, nor defert me!
Th' all-ruling Goodnefs may relieve us ftill.

ELEONORA.

Edward! I tremble! terror feizes on me!
Thro' the rent veil of yon furrounding fky,
I had a glimpfe, I faw th' eternal world,
They call, they urge me hence--Yes, I obey.
But O forgive me, Heaven! if 'tis with pain,
With agonies, I tear my foul from his!

VOL. IV.   D   EDWARD

EDWARD.

Heavens! what I suffer!—How thy plaintive voice
Shoots anguish thro' my soul!

ELEONORA.

　　　　　　　Some Power unseen—
Thy hand, my *Edward*—some dark power unseen
Is dragging me away—O yet a little,
A little, spare me!—Ah! how shall I leave
My weeping friends, my husband and my children?

EDWARD.

Unhappy friends! O greatly wretched husband!
And O poor careless orphans, who not feel
The depth of your misfortune!

ELEONORA.

　　　　　　　Lay me down;
Soft, lay me down—my powers are all dissolv'd—
A little forward bend me—Oh!

EDWARD.

　　　　　　　Oh Heav'n!
How that soft frame is torn with cruel pangs!
Pangs robb'd from me!

ELEONORA.

　　　　　　　'Tis thence they borrow ease—
My children! O my children! you no more
Have now a mother; now, alas! no more
Have you a mother. O my hapless children!

EDWARD.

What do! hear! What desolating words
Are these? more bitter than a thousand deaths!

2　　　　　　　　　　　. Death

Death to my foul! Call up thy failing fpirit,
And leave me not to mifery and ruin!

ELEONORA.

Edward, I feel an interval of eafe:
And, ere I die, have fomething to impart
That will relieve my fufferings.

EDWARD.

Speak, my foul!
Speak thy defire: I live but to fulfil it.

ELEONORA.

Thou feeft in what a hopelefs ftate I lie,
I who this morning rofe in pride of youth,
High-blooming, promis'd many happy years.
I die for thee, I felf-devoted die.
Think not, from this, that I repent my vow:
Or that, with little vanity, I boaft it:
No; what I did from unrepenting love
I chearful did, from love that knows no fear,
No pain, no weak remiffion of its ardour.
And what, alas! what was it but the dictate
Of honour and of duty? nay, 'twas felfifh,
To fave me from unfufferable pain,
From dragging here a wretched life without thee.
Two fears yet ftand betwixt my foul and peace.
One is for thee, left thou difturb my grave
With tears of wild defpair. Grieve not like thofe
Who have no hope. We yet fhall meet again;
We ftill are in a kind Creator's hand;
Eternal Goodnefs reigns. Befides, this parting,
This parting, *Edward*, muft have come at laft,

When

When years of friendſhip had, perhaps, exalted
Our love, if that can be, to keener anguiſh.
Think what thy ſtation, what thy fame demanded;
Nor yield thy virtue even to worthy paſſions.
My other care—my other care is idle——
From that thy equal tenderneſs with mine,
Thy love and generoſity ſecure me.
Our children——

EDWARD.

Yes, I penetrate thy fear.
But hear me, dying ſweetneſs! On this hand,
This cold pale hand I vow, our children never,
Shall never call another by the name
Sacred to thee; my *Eleonora's* children
Shall never feel the hateful power thou fear'ſt.
As one in life, ſo death cannot divide us.
Nor high deſcent, nor beauty, nought that woman,
In her unbounded vanity of heart,
Can wiſh, ſhall ever tempt my faith from thee.
Shall ever, ſaid I? -Piteous boaſt indeed!
O nothing *can!*—I ſhould be groſs of heart,
Taſteleſs and dull as earth, to think with patience,
Without abhorrence, of a ſecond *Hymen.*
Where can I find ſuch beauty? Where ſuch grace,
The ſoul of beauty? where ſuch winning charms?
Where ſuch a ſoft divinity of goodneſs?
Such faith? ſuch love? ſuch tenderneſs unequal'd?
Such all that Heaven could give--to make me wretched!
Talk not of comfort—Into what a gulph
A lone abyſs of miſery I fall,

The moment that I lofe thee—Oh! I know not!
I dare not think!—But thefe unhappy orphans—
Ah the dire caufe that makes it double duty——
Shall now be doubly mine ; to fhelter them,
'Thefe pledges of our love, I will attempt
To brave the horrors of loath'd life without thee.

ELEONORA.

Enough! it is enough! On this condition
Receive them from my hands.

EDWARD.

Dear hands! dear gift!
Dear, precious, dying, miferable gift!
With tranfport once receiv'd, but now with anguifh!

ELEONORA.

All-foft'ning time will heal my woes. The dead
Soon leave the paffions of the living free.

EDWARD.

Detefted life!—O take me, take me with thee!

ELEONORA.

No, *Edward*, live ; or elfe I die in vain. .

EDWARD.

Raife, raife, my *Eleonora*, thy fweet eyes,
Once more behold thy children—

ELEONORA.

Oh!—'Tis darknefs—
A deadly weight—— ——

EDWARD.

Thou leav'ft me then for ever!

ELEONORA.

Where am I ?—Ah!—a tenant ftill to pain.

The

'The quivering flame of life leaps up a little.
Meantime, my *Edward*, 'tis my laſt requeſt,
That thou wouldſt leave me, while I yet enjoy
A parting gleam of thought—Leave me to Heaven!—
Gloſter—farewel—Be careful of the prince—
Attend him hence—and double now thy friendſhip!

EDWARD.

Barbarian! off!—Ah! whither would'ſt thou drag me!

GLOSTER.

My lord, in pity to the princeſs—

EDWARD.

Oh!

ELEONORA.

Farewel! farewel!—Receive my laſt adieu,
Edward! my deareſt lord! farewel for ever!

EDWARD.

O word of horror!—Can I?—No! I cannot!
There, take me, lead me, hurl me to perdition!

S C E N E VI.

ELEONORA, DARAXA THEALD, *Attendants.*

ELEONORA.

'Tis paſt, the bitterneſs of death is paſt——
  Alas! *Daraxa*, I can ne'er requite
Thy generous cares for me. Thou art the cauſe
My *Edward* lives, my children have a father,

Thy

Thy heaven-infpir'd propofal—Tell him, *Theald*,
That, in the troubled moments of our parting,
I had forgot to beg he would reftore
Th' *Arabian* princefs to her friends and country—
Thy hand—This fure, howe'er in faith we differ,
Humanity, the foul of all religion,
May well permit.

DARAXA.
By Virtue's facred fire!
Our paradife, the garden of the bleft,
Ne'er fmil'd upon a purer foul than thine.
  For me, think not of me ; fuch are my woes,
That I difdain all care, deteft relief.:
My name is trod in duft ; thine beams for-ever,
The richeft gem that crowns the worth of woman.

ELEONORA.
The guilt of *Selim* cannot ftain thy virtues :
It rather lends them luftre—Bear me back
My dear attendants : and good *Theald*, come,
Come, aid my mounting foul to fpring away,
From the lov'd fetters of this kindred clay.

The End of the Third Act.

D 4 ACT

ACT IV. SCENE I.

*'*T H E A L D, *and a* Gentleman *belonging to him.*

THEALD.

TO me a dervife? Thro' the furious camp,
 Yet raging at the perfidy of *Selim*,
How did he fafely pafs?

GENTLEMAN.

    Sir, he had fallen
A victim to their vengeance: but he told them,
His life was of importance to the prince,
That he who ftruck him ftabb'd the heart of *Edward.*
This ftay'd their rage; then, after a ftrict fearch,
They let him pafs thro' ranks of glaring eyes.
 I have befides to fay, an *Englifh* fhip
And one from *Italy* are juft arriv'd:
The firft brings great difpatches to prince *Edward*;
The other, *holy father*, thefe to you. [*Kneeling.*

THEALD.

Go, bid this dervife enter.

          S C E N E

SCENE II.

THEALD: *he opens and looks on the Dispatches.*

Awful Heaven!
Great ruler of the various heart of man!
Since thou haft rais'd me to conduct thy church,
Without the bafe cabal too often practis'd,
Beyond my wifh, my thought, give me the lights,
The virtues which that facred truft requires:
A loving, lov'd, unterrifying power,
Such as becomes a father: humble wifdom;
Plain, primitive fincerity; kind zeal,
For truth and virtue rather than opinions;
And, above all, the charitable foul
Of healing peace and chriftian moderation.——
The *dervife* comes.

SCENE III.

THEALD, SELIM *difguifed as a Dervife.*

THEALD.
With me, what would'ft thou, dervife?
SELIM.
The princefs *Eleonora* lives fhe ftill?

D 5

THEALD.

THEALD.

She lives, and that is all.

SELIM.

Allah be prais'd !
Then lives the honour of the brightning name
Of *Saracen* and *Muſſulman.*

THEALD.

How, dervife ?
What can wipe out the horror of this deed ?

SELIM.

The deed was execrable ; but my hand
This inſtant ſhall prevent its dire effect.
I bring a certain remedy for poiſon ;
Nor can it come too late, while wandering life
Yet, with faint impulſe, ſtirs along the veins.

THEALD.

Ha ! dervife, art thou ſure of what thou ſay'ſt ?

SELIM.

Chriſtian, I am ; and therefore am I here.
Haſte, lead me to the princefs : tho' ſhe lay
Even in the laſt extremity, tho' call'd
By the fierce angel who compels the dead,
Yet bold experience gives me room to hope.
Oft have I ſeen its vital touch diffufe
New vigour thro' the poiſon'd ſtreams of life,
When almoſt ſettled into dead ſtagnation ;
Swift as a ſouthern gale unbinds the flood.
Say, wilt thou truſt me with the trial, chriſtian.

THEALD.

THEALD.

Thou know'ft, we have great reafon for diftruft;
But fear in thofe who can no longer hope,
Were idle and abfurd.

SELIM.

Bright Heaven! what fear?
Is there a flave of fuch inhuman bafenefs
To add frefh outrage to a dying princefs?
For virtue dying? look into my eye:
Does one weak ray there fhun the keeneft gaze?
Say, doft thou there behold fo foul a bottom?

THEALD.

No; feeming truth and generous candour fhine
In what thou fay'ft. Come, follow me, good dervife.

SCENE IV.

THEALD, SELIM *difguifed*, DARAXA.

DARAXA.

At laft, through various pangs the dying princefs
Sees the delivering moment, and demands
Thy prefence, reverend chriftian.

THEALD.

Dervife, come.
Forbid it Heaven this aid fhould be too late!

D 6   SCENE

SCENE V.

DARAXA.

Heaven! can it be! the very face of *Selim!*
'Tis he himself—I know him, 'tis the fultan;
And, as he fhot athwart me, from his eye
Flafh'd the proud lightning of affronted virtue.
He muft be innocent; his being here
Is radiant proof he muft—O weak DARAXA!
What man of virtue more would deign to lodge
His image in thy breaft? Ah! what avails
The light unfounded love, the treacherous friendfhip,
That, with inhuman cowardice, gives up
A worthy man, to infamy and flander?
They talk'd of aid—what aid?

                    [*A cry heard within.*
                    Alas! 'tis paft!

Death muft be in that cry.   O let me fly
To fnatch one parting look; but fee the prince
Rous'd by the founds of forrow this way comes.
Unhappy prince! I venerate his tears—
O gracious Allah! pity and fupport him.   [*Exit.*

SCENE VI.

EDWARD.

That cry was death: Alas! she is no more!
The matchless *Eleonora* is no more!—
Where am I?—Heavens!—Ah! what a hideous defart
Is now this world, this blasted world around me!
O sun, I hate thee, I abhor thy light,
That shews not *Eleonora!* Earth, thy joy,
Thy sweetness all is fled, all all that made
Thy ways to me delightful, *Eleonora!*
O *Eleonora!* perish'd *Eleonora!*
For ever lost!—That tent! ah me! that tent!

> [*Going into the tent starts back.*

I dare not enter there. There death displays
His utmost terrors—Pale and lifeless, there,
She lies, whose looks were love, whose beauty smil'd
The sweet effulgence of endearing virtue—
And here I last beheld her—Ay, and how,
And how beheld her?—The remorseless image
Will haunt me to the grave—I see her suffering,
With female softness yet to pain superior,
Fearful and bold at once with the strong hand
Of mighty love constraining feeble nature,
To steal me from affliction—Let me fly
This fatal ground—But whither shall I fly?
To *England*—O I cannot bear the thought
Of e'er returning to that country more!

That

That country, witnefs of our happy days,
Where at each ftep remember'd blifs will fting
My foul to anguifh. I already hear
Malice exclaim, nay, blufhing Valour figh:
Where is thy princefs? where the wifh of thoufands?
The charm, the tranfport of the public eye?
Bafe prince! And art thou not afham'd to bring
No trophy home but *Eleonora's* corfe?——
The grave too is fhut up, that laft retreat
Of wretched mortals—Yes, my word is pafs'd,
To *Eleonora* pafs'd. Our orphan children
Bind me to life—O dear, O dangerous paffions!
The valiant, in himfelf, what can he fuffer?
Or what does he regard his fingle woes?
But when, alas, he multiplies himfelf
To dearer felves, to the lov'd tender fair,
To thofe whofe blifs, whofe beings hang upon him,
To helplefs children! then, O then! he feels
The point of mifery feftering in his heart,
And weakly weeps his fortune like a coward.
Such, fuch am I! undone!——

SCENE

SCENE VII.

EDWARD, GLOSTER.

EDWARD.
My lord of *Gloster*,
I thought my orders were to be alone.
GLOSTER.
Forgive my fond intrusion—But I cannot
Be so regardless of thy welfare, *Edward*,
As to obey these orders.
EDWARD.
But they shall,
Shall be obey'd—I will enjoy my sorrows,
All that is left me now.
GLOSTER.
The more thy grief,
Just in its cause but frantic in degree,
Seeks aggravating solitude, the more
It suits my love and duty to attend thee;
To try to sooth—
EDWARD.
Away! thou never shalt.
Not all that idle wisdom can suggest,
All the vain talk of proud unfeeling reason,
Shall rob me of one tear.
GLOSTER.
Of Nature's tears
I would

I would not rob thee: they invigorate virtue,
Soften, at once, and fortify the heart;
But when they rife to fpeak this defperate language,
They then grow tears of weaknefs; yes—

EDWARD.

I care not!

Weaknefs, whate'er they be, I will indulge them,
Will, in defpite of thee and all mankind,.
Devote my joylefs days for ever to them.

GLOSTER.

Reafon and virtue then are empty names?

EDWARD.

Hence! leave me to my fate—You have undone me;
You have made fhipwreck of my peace, among you,
My happinefs and honour; and I now
Roam the detefted world, a carelefs wretch!

GLOSTER.

Thy honour yet is fafe, how long I know not,.
For full it drives upon the rocks of paffion.
O all ye pitying Powers that rule mankind!
Who fo unworthy but may proudly deck him
With this fair-weather virtue, that exults,
Glad, o'er the fummer main? The tempeft comes,
The rough winds rage aloud; when from the helm
This virtue fhrinks, and in a corner lies
Lamenting.—Heavens! if privileg'd from trial,.
How cheap a thing were virtue!

EDWARD..

Do—infult me—

Rail,.

Rail, fpare me not—rail, *Glofter*, all the world—
But know, mean time, thou canft not make me feel
        thee—
I have no more connection with mankind.

GLOSTER.

Infult thee, *Edward?* Do thefe tears infult thee?
Thefe old man's tears!—Friendfhip, my prince, can
        weep,
As well as love—But while I weep thy fortune,
Let me not weep thy virtue funk beneath it—
Thou haft no more connection with mankind?
Put off thy craving fenfes, the deep wants
And infinite dependencies of nature;
Put off that ftrongeft paffion of the foul,
Soul of the foul, love to fociety;
Put off all gratitude for what is paft,
All generous hope of what is yet to come;
Put off each fenfe of honour and of duty:
Then ufe this language—Let me tell thee, *Edward,*
Thou haft connections with mankind, and great ones,
Thou know'ft not of; connections! that might roufe
The fmalleft fpark of honour in thy breaft,
To wide-awaken'd life and fair ambition.

EDWARD.

What doft thou mean?

GLOSTER.

      What mean?—this day, in *England,*
How many afk of *Paleftine* their king,
Edward their king?—Read thefe—

                    EDWARD.

EDWARD, *opening the difpatches.*

O *Glofter !—Glofter !—*

Alas ! my royal father is no more !
The gentleft of mankind, the moft abus'd !
Of gracious nature, a fit foil for virtues,
'Till there his creatures fow'd their flattering lies,
And made him—No, not all their curfed arts
Could ever make him infolent or cruel.
O my deluded father ! Little joy
Had'ft thou in life, led from thy real good,
And genuine glory, from thy people's love,
That nobleft aim of kings, by fmiling traitors.
    Thus weak of heart, thus defolate of foul,
Ah, how unfit am I, with fteady hand,
To rule a troubled ftate !—She, fhe is gone,
Softner of care, the dear reward of toil,
The fource of virtue ! She, who to a crown
Had lent new fplendor, who had grac'd a throne·
Like the fweet feraph Mercy tempering Juftice.
O *Eleonora !* any life with thee,
The plaineft could have charm'd : but pomp and
        pleafure,
All that a loving people can beftow,
By thee unfhar'd, will only ferve to fret
The wounds of woe, and make me more unhappy !

GLOSTER.

Now is the time, now lift thy foul to virtue !
Behold a crifis, fent by Heaven, to fave thee.
Whate'er, my prince, can touch, or can command,
Can quicken or exalt the heart of man,

                                        Now

Now speaks to thine—Thy children claim their father,
Nay, more than father, claim their double parent;
For such thy promise was to *Eleonora :*
Thy subjects claim their king, thy troops their chief:
The manes of thy anceftors confign
Their long-defcended glory to thy hands;
And thy dejected country calls upon thee
To fave her, raife her, to reftore her honour,
To fpread her fure dominion o'er the deep,
And bid her yet arife the fcourge of *France.*
Angels themfelves might envy thee the joy,
That waits thy will, of doing general good :
Of fpreading virtue, chearing lonely worth;
Of dafhing down the proud ; of guarding arts,
The facred rights of induftry and freedom;
Of making a whole generous people happy.
O *Edward ! Edward !* the moft piercing tranfports
Of the beft love can never equal thefe !
And need I add—Thy *Eleonora's* death
Calls out for vengeance ? ——

EDWARD.
Ha !
GLOSTER.
If thou, indeed,
Doft honour thus her memory, then fhew it,
Not by foft tears and womanifh complaints,
But fhew it like a man !——

EDWARD.
I will !

GLOSTER.

GLOSTER.

Yon towers!—

EDWARD.

'Tis true!

GLOSTER.

Yon guilty towers!—

EDWARD.

Infult us ftill!

GLOSTER.

The murderer of thy princefs riots there!—

EDWARD.

But fhall not long!—Thou art my better genius,
Thou brave old man! thou haft recall'd my virtue—
I was benumb'd with forrow—what—or where—
I know not—never to have thought of this.
Bright Virtue, welcome! vigour of the mind!
The flame from Heaven that lights up higher being!
Thrice welcome! with thy noble fervant Anger,
And juft Revenge—Hence, let us to the camp,
And there transfufe our foul into the troops.
This fultan's blood will eafe my fever'd breaft.
Yes, I will take fuch vengeance on this city,
That all mankind fhall turn their eyes to *Jaffa*;
And as they fee her turrets funk in duft,
Shall learn to dread the terrors of the juft.

The End of the Fourth Act.

A C T

ACT V. SCENE I.

SELIM.

O My *Daraxa!* thou haſt charm'd my ſoul!
This reconciling interview has ſooth'd
My troubled boſom into tender joy:
As when the ſpring firſt, on the ſoften'd top
Of *Lebanon*, unbinds her lovely treſſes,
And ſhakes her blooming ſweets from *Carmel*'s brow—
It only now remains to ſee the prince.——

SCENE II.

SELIM, THEALD.

THEALD.

I ſought thee, worthy dervife.

SELIM.

Reverend chriſtian,
My toiling thoughts can find no fix'd repoſe,
'Till the wrong'd ſultan's vindicated honour

Shine

Shine out as bright as yon unfully'd fky.
Conduct me to the prince—I claim that juſtice.—
It ſtings my conſcious ſoul with ſick impatience,
To think what *Selim* ſuffers. For a man,
Who loves the ways of truth and open virtue,
To lye beneath the burning imputation
Of baſeneſs and of crimes—ſuch horrid crimes!—
O 'tis a keen unſufferable torment!
Come, let me then diſcharge this other part
Of my commiſſion.

THEALD.

That thou ſoon ſhalt do.
He ſtrait will come this way, the king of *England*,
Such now he is.   Mean time, 'tis fit to tell thee,
He muſt be manag'd gently ; for his paſſions
Are all abroad, in wild confuſion hurl'd :
The winds, the floods, and lightning mix together.
I need not ſay how little, in this uproar,
Avails the broken thwarted light of reaſon.

SELIM.

Fear not.—I truſt in innocence, and truth.

THEALD.

He cannot long delay, for, as I enter'd,
I ſaw him parting from the hurried camp,
That lighten'd wide around him : burniſh'd helms,
And glittering ſpears, and ardent thronging ſoldiers,
Demanding all the ſignal, when to ſtorm
Theſe walls devoted to their vengeance.—

                                    SELIM.

SELIM.

Ha!

Then let us quickly find him—But he comes.

SCENE III.

SELIM, THEALD, EDWARD, GLOSTER.

EDWARD.

Whence is it those barbarians, here again,
Those base, those murdering cowards, dare be seen?
What new accurs'd attempt is now on foot?
What new affaffination?—Start not, dervife,
Tinge not thy caitiff cheek with red'ning honour.
What thou !--Doft thou pretend to feel reproach?
Art thou not of a fhamelefs race of people,
Harden'd in arts of cruelty and blood,
Perfidious all? Yes, have you not profan'd
The faith of nations, broke the holy tie
That binds the families of earth together,
That gives even foes to meet with generous truft,
And teaches war fecurity? Your prince,
Your prince has done it! And you fhould hereafter
Be hunted from your dens like favage beafts,
Be crufh'd like ferpents!

THEALD.

Sir, this dervife comes,
To clear the fultan *Selim* from that crime,

Which

Which you, with ftrong appearance, charge upon him.

EDWARD.

Appearance, *Theald!* with unqueftion'd proof.
Doubtlefs the villain would be glad to change
The courfe by Nature fix'd, enjoy his crimes
Without their evil—But he fhall not fcape me!

SELIM.

If, king of *England*, in this weighty matter,
On which depends the weal and life of thoufands,
You love and feek the truth, let reafon judge,
Cool, fteady, quiet, and difpaffion'd reafon.
For never yet, fince the proud felfifh race
Of men began to jar, did paffion give,
Nor ever can it give, a right decifion.

EDWARD.

Reafon has judg'd, and paffion fhall chaftife,
Shall make you howl, ye cowards of the *Eaft!*
What can be clearer? This vile prince of *Jaffa!*
This infamy of princes! fends a ruffian,
By his own hand and feal commiffion'd, fends him,
To treat of peace: and, as I read his letters,
The villain ftabs me—This, if this wants light,
There is no certainty in human reafon;
If this not fhines with all-convincing truth,
Yon fun is dark—And yet thefe cowards come
With lying fhifts, and low elufive arts—
O, it inflames my anger into madnefs!
This added infult on our underftanding,
This treacherous attempt to fteal away

The

The only joy and treaſure of my life,
Sweet ſacred vengeance for my murder'd princeſs.

SELIM.

The curſed wretch who did aſſail thy life,
O king of *England*, was indeed an envoy
Sent by the prince of *Jaffa:* This we own,
But then he was an execrable bigot,
Who, for ſuch horrid purpoſes, had crept
Into the cheated ſultan's court and ſervice,
As by the traitor's papers we have learn'd.
For know, there lives, upon the craggy cliffs
Of wild *Phenician* mountains, a dire race,
A nation of aſſaſſins.   Dreadful zeal,
Fierce and intolerant of all religion
That differs from their own, is the black ſoul
Of that infernal ſtate.   Soon as their chief,
The Old Man (ſo they ſtile him) of the mountains,
Gives out his baleful will, however fell,
However wicked and abhorr'd it be,
Tho' cloth'd in danger, the moſt cruel death,
They, ſwift and ſilent, glide thro' every land,
As fly the gloomy miniſters of vengeance,
Famine and plague; they lie for years conceal'd,
Make light of oaths, nay, ſometimes change religion,
And never fail to execute his orders.
Of theſe the villain was, theſe ruffian ſaints,
The curſe of earth, the terror of mankind :
And thy engagement, prince, in this cruſado,
That was the reaſon whence they ſought thy life.

EDWARD.

False, false as hell! the lye of guilty fear!
You all are bigots, robbers, ruffians all!
It is the very genius of your nation.
Vindictive rage, the thirst of blood consumes you:
You live by rapine, thence your empire rose;
And your religion is a mere pretence
To rob and murder in the name of Heaven.

SELIM.

Be patient, prince, be more humane and just.
You have your virtues, have your vices too;
And we have ours. The liberal hand of Nature
Has not created us, nor any nation,
Beneath the blessed canopy of heaven,
Of such malignant clay, but each may boast
Their native virtues, and their maker's bounty.
You call us bigots.—O! canst thou with that
Reproach us, christian prince? What brought thee
              hither?
What else but bigotry? What dost thou here?
What else but persecute?—the truth is great,
Greater than thou, and I will give it way;
Even thou thyself, in all thy rage, wilt hear it—
From their remotest source, these holy wars
What have they breath'd but bigotry and rapine?
Did not the first *Crusaders,* when their zeal
Should have shone out the purest, did they not,
Led by the frantic hermit who began
The murderous trade, thro' their own countries spread
The woes their vice could not reserve for ours?

                                    Tho'

Tho' this exceeds the purport of my meſſage ;
Yet muſt I thus inſulted in my country,
Inſulted in religion, bid thee think,
O king of *England*, on the different conduct
Of *Saracens* and *Chriſtians*, when beneath
Your pious *Godfrey*, in the firſt cruſado,
Jeruſalem was ſack'd, and when beneath
Our generous *Saladin* it was retaken——
O hideous ſcene ! my ſoul within me ſhrinks,
Abhorrent, from the view ! — Twelve thouſand
    wretches,
Receiv'd to mercy, void of all defence,
Truſting to plighted faith, to purchas'd ſafety,
Behold theſe naked wretches, in cold blood.
Men, women, children, murder'd, baſely murder'd !
The holy temple, which you came to reſcue,
Regorges with the barbarous profanation.
The ſtreets run diſmal torrents. Drown'd in blood
The very ſoldier ſickens at his carnage.
Couldſt thou, O ſun, behold the blaſting ſight,
And lift again thy ſacred eye on mortals ?
A ruthleſs race ! Who can do this, can do it,
To pleaſe the general Father of mankind !
While nobler *Saladin* ——

           EDWARD.

        Away ! be gone !
With thee, vile derviſe, what have I to do ?
I loſe my hour of vengeance, I debaſe me,
To hold this talk with thee.

         E 2   SELIM.

SELIM.

> While truth and reafon
Speak from my tongue, vile dervife as I am
Yet am I greater than the higheft monarch,
Who, from blind fury, grows the flave of paffion.
Befides, I come to juftify a prince,
Howe'er in other qualities below thee,
In love of goodnefs, truth, humanity,
And honour, Sir, thy equal;—yes, thy equal!—

EDWARD.

What? how? compare me with a damn'd affaffin?
A matchlefs villain!—Ha! prefumptuous dervife!
Thou gnaw'ft thy quivering lip—A fmother'd paffion
Shakes thro' thy frame.—What villany is that
Thou dar'ft not utter?—Wert thou not a wretch,
Protected by thy habit, this right hand
Should crufh thee into atoms—Hence! away!
Go tell thy mafter that I hold him bafe,
Beyond the power of words to fpeak his bafenefs!
A coward! an affaffinating coward!
And when I once have dragg'd him from his city,
Which I will ftraitway do—I then will make him,
In all the gall and bitternefs of guilt,
Grinding the vengeful fteel betwixt his teeth,
Will make the traitor own it.

SELIM, *difcovering himfelf.*

> Never!

EDWARD.

> Ha!

SELIM.

SELIM.

Thou canſt not, haughty monarch :—I am he!
I am this *Selim !* this inſulted *Selim !*
Yet clear as day, and will confound thy paſſion.

EDWARD.

Thou *Selim !*

SELIM.

I.

EDWARD.

Was ever guilt ſo bold ?

SELIM.

Did ever innocence deſcend to fear ?

EDWARD.

This bears ſome ſhew of honour.   Wilt thou then
Decide it by the ſword ?

SELIM.

I will do more——

EDWARD.

How more ?

SELIM.

Decide it by ſuperior reaſon.

EDWARD.

No weak evaſions !——

SELIM.

If I not convince thee,
If by thyſelf I am not of this crime
Acquitted, then I grant thee thy demand.
Nay more, yon yielded city ſhall be thine :
For know, hot prince, I ſhould diſdain a throne,

E. 3   I could

I could not fill with honour. Were I guilty,
I fhould not tremble at thy threatning voice;
No, 'tis myfelf I fear.

EDWARD.
What fhall I think?

SELIM.
Hear but one witnefs, and I afk no more,
To clear my name. The witnefs is a woman.
Her looks are truth; fair uncorrupted faith
Beams from her eyes. Thou ne'er canft doubt fuch
    beauty;
For 'tis th' expreffion of a fpotlefs foul.

EDWARD.
Curfe on thy mean luxurious eaftern arts
Of cowardice! Thou would'ft feduce my vengeance—
But I deteft all beauty—Barbarous fultan!
Ah! thou haft murder'd beauty! thy fell crime—
Hafte, *Glofter*, hafte—in fight of camp and city,
Prepare the lifts—Now fhow thyfelf a prince,
Or die in fhameful tortures like a flave.

SELIM.
I came not hither or to dread thy wrath,
Or court thy mercy.

GLOSTER.
        Sir, you cannot juftly
Refufe him his demand. The fervent foul
Of undiffembled innocence, methinks,
Is felt in what he fays. Firft hear this perfon;
And if fhe gives not full conviction, then,

                        Have

Have then recourse to what should always be
The last appeal of reasonable beings,
Brute force.

EDWARD.

Well then, conduct her hither, sultan——

[Selim goes out.

Ah! my disorder'd mind! from thought to thought,
Uncertain, toss'd, the wreck of stormy passion!
This rage a while supports me; but I feel
It will desert me soon, and I again
Shall soon relapse to misery and weakness.
O Eleonora! little didst thou think,
How deeply wretched thy dire gift of life
Would make me!

SCENE IV.

EDWARD, GLOSTER, THEALD; to them SELIM
conducting ELEONORA, DARAXA.

SELIM.

Raise thy eyes, O king of England,
To the bright witness of my blameless honour.

EDWARD.

No; beauty shall no more engage my eyes,
It shall no more profane the shrine devoted.

E 4   To

To the fweet image of my *Eleonora!*
Let her declare her knowledge in this matter.

ELEONORA.

Will not my *Edward* blefs me with a look?

EDWARD.

What angel borrows *Eleonora*'s voice!—
O thou pale fhade of her I weep for ever!
Permit me thus to worfhip thee—Thou art!—
Amazing Heaven!—Thou art my *Eleonora!*
My *Eleonora*'s felf! my dear, my true,
My living *Eleonora!*—What—to whom
Owe I this miracle? this better life?—
Oppreffive joy!—owe I my *Eleonora?*

ELEONORA.

To him, that generous prince, who put his life,
His honour on the defperate rifque to fave me,
When in the arms of death—Depriv'd of voice,
Of motion, and of fenfe, benumb'd I lay,
My frighted train around me thought me dead,
And fill'd the tent with cries; my heart alone
Still feebly beat; but foon the poifon's force
Had driv'n out life from that its laft retreat;
If in the moment of approaching fate,
He, like my guardian angel, had not brought
An antidote of wond'rous power, by which
I am to light reftor'd—to thee, my *Edward!*

EDWARD.

Did he, did he preferve thee! He, whom thus
I have with fuch inhuman pride infulted!

O blind,

O blind, O brutish, O injurious rage!
They, they are wife, who, when they feel thy madnefs,
Seal up their lips. And canft thou then forgive me,
Thou who haft o'er me gain'd that nobleft triumph,
The triumph of humanity?—Thou canft.
'Tis eafier for the generous to forgive
Than for offence to afk it.

SELIM.

Ufe not, prince,
So harfh a word. More than-forgive, I love
Thy noble heat, thy beautiful diforder.
O! I am too much man, I feel, myfelf,
Too much the charming force of human paffions,
E'er to pretend, with fupercilious brow,
With proud affected virtue, to difdain them.

EDWARD.

How? generous fultan, how fhall I requite thee?
Here—Take thy lov'd *Daraxa*, whom I meant
To have reftor'd, when this misfortune happen'd;
But fecret-working Heaven ordain'd her ftay,
To fave us all.

SELIM.

Wert thou the lord of earth,
Thou could'ft not give me more!—my dear *Daraxa*!

EDWARD.

Hence to the camp, my *Glofter*—Bid the foldiers
Forfake the trenches—Let unbounded joy
Reign, fearlefs, o'er the mingled camp and city—

E. 5. Go,

Go, tell my faithful foldiers, that their queen
My *Eleonora* lives! A prize beyond
The chance of war to give! She lives to foften
My too imperious temper, and to make them,
To make my people happy!—O my foul!
What love e'er equal'd thine? O deareft! beft!
Pride of thy fex! inimitable goodnefs!
Whenever woman henceforth fhall be prais'd
For conjugal affection, men will fay,
There fhine the virtues of an *Eleonora!*
Tranfporting blifs!—How bountiful is Heaven!
Depreffing often, but to raife us more.
Let never thofe defpair who follow virtue.
Love—gratitude—divide me—Once more, fultan,
Forgive me, pardon my miftaken zeal,
That left my country, crofs'd the ftormy feas,
To war with thee, brave prince, to war with honour.
Now that my paffions give me leave to think;
The hand of Heaven appears in what I fuffer'd,
My erring zeal has fuffer'd by a zealot.

SELIM.

It does, O king. And, venerable chriftian,
I know thy moderation will excufe me.
But fince by ruling Wifdom (who unweigh'd,
Unmeant, does nought) men are fo various made,
So various turn'd, that in opinions, they
Muft blindly think, or take a different way;

In

In fpite of force, fince judgment will be free;
Then let us in this righteous mean agree:
Let holy rage, let perfecution ceafe;
Let the head argue, but the heart be peace;.
' Let all mankind in love of what is right,
In virtue and humanity, unite.

The End of the Fifth Act.

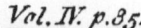

G.V. Neijt Sc.

Tancred *and* Sigismunda.

Tancred and Sigismunda.

A

TRAGEDY,

TO HIS

ROYAL HIGHNESS

FREDERICK,
Prince of . *Wales*.

S I R,

THE honour your ROYAL HIGH-
NESS has done me in the protection you was pleafed to give to this tragedy, emboldens me to lay it now at your
feet, and beg your permiffion to publifh
it under your Royal patronage. The favouring and protecting of letters has been,
in all ages and countries, one diftinguifh-
ing mark of a great prince; and that with
good reafon, not only as it fhews a juftnefs
of tafte, and elevation of mind, but as the

influence

influence of fuch a protection, by exciting good writers to labour with more emulation in the improvement of their feveral talents, not a little contributes to the embellifhment and inftruction of fociety. But of all the different fpecies of writing, none has fuch an effect upon the lives and manners of men, as the dramatic; and therefore, that of all others moft deferves the attention of princes; who, by a judicious approbation of fuch pieces as tend to promote all public and private virtue, may more than by any coercive methods fecure the purity of the ftage, and in confequence thereof greatly advance the morals and politenefs of their people. How eminently Your ROYAL HIGHNESS has always extended your favour and patronage to every art and fcience, and in a particular manner to dramatic performances, is too well known to the world for me to mention it here. Allow me only to wifh, that what I have now the honour to offer to your

ROYAL

DEDICATION.

ROYAL HIGHNESS, may be judged not unworthy of your protection, at leaft in the *Sentiments* which it inculcates. A warm and grateful fenfe of your goodnefs to me, makes me defirous to feize every occafion of declaring in public, with what profound refpect and dutiful attachment, I am,

SIR,

Your ROYAL HIGHNESS's

Moft obliged,

moft obedient, and

moft devoted Servant,

JAMES THOMSON.

ADVERTISEMENT.

THIS play is considerably shortened in the performance; but I hope it will not be disagreeable to the Reader to see it as it was at first written; there being a great difference betwixt a play in the closet, and upon the stage.

PROLOGUE.

BOLD *is the man! who, in this nicer age,*
   Presumes to tread the chaste corrected page.
Now, with gay tinsel arts, we can no more
Conceal the want of Nature's sterling ore.
Our spells are vanish'd, broke our magic wand,
That us'd to waft you over sea and land.
Before your light the fairy people fade,
The demons fly—The ghost itself is laid.
In vain of martial scenes the loud alarms,
The mighty prompter thundering out to arms,
The playhouse posse clattering from afar,
The close-wedg'd battle, and the din of war.
Now, even the senate seldom we convene;
The yawning fathers nod behind the scene.
Your taste rejects the glittering false sublime,
To sigh in metaphor, and die in rhime.
High rant is tumbled from his gallery throne:
Description, dreams—nay, similies are gone.

   What shall we then? to please you how devise
Whose judgment sits not in your ears and eyes?
Thrice happy! could we catch great Shakespear's *art,*
To trace the deep recesses of the heart;
His simple plain sublime, to which is given
To strike the soul with darted flame from heaven:
Could we awake soft Otway's *tender woe,*
The pomp of verse and golden lines of Rowe.

   We to your hearts apply: let them attend;
Before their silent candid bar we bend.
If warm'd, they listen, 'tis our noblest praise;
If cold, they wither all the muse's bays.

                         The

The Persons represented.

TANCRED, Count of *Leece*,   Mr. *Garrick.*

MATTEO SIFFREDI, Lord High Chancellor of *Sicily*, } Mr. *Sheridan.*

EARL *Osmond*, Lord High Constable of *Sicily*, } Mr. *Delane.*

RODOLPHO, Friend to *Tancred*, and Captain of the Guards, } Mr. *Havard.*

SIGISMUNDA, Daughter of *Siffredi*, Mrs. *Cibber.*

LAURA, Sister of *Rodolpho*, and Friend to *Sigismunda*, } Miss *Budgel.*

Barons, Officers, Guards, &c.

SCENE, *The City of* Palermo *in* Sicily.

Tancred and *Sigismunda.*

A

TRAGEDY.

ACT I. SCENE I.

SIGISMUNDA, LAURA.

SIGISMUNDA.

AH fatal day to *Sicily!* The king
Approaches his laſt moments?

LAURA.

So 'tis fear'd.

SIGISMUNDA.

The death of thoſe diſtinguiſh'd by their ſtation,
But by their virtue more, awakes the mind

To

To folemn dread, and ftrikes a faddening awe:
Not that we grieve for them, but for ourfelves,
Left to the toil of life—And yet the beft
Are, by the playful children of this world,
At once forgot, as they had never been.

   Laura, 'tis faid—the heart is fometimes charged
With a prophetic fadnefs: Such, methinks,
Now hangs on mine. The king's approaching death
Suggefts a thoufand fears.   What troubles thence
May throw the ftate once more into confufion,
What fudden changes in my father's houfe
May rife, and part me from my deareft *Tancred*,
Alarms my thought.

LAURA.

     The fears of love-fick fancy!
Perverfely bufy to torment itfelf.
But be affur'd, your father's fteady friendfhip,
Join'd to a certain genius, that commands,
Not kneels to fortune, will fupport and cherifh,
Here in the public eye of *Sicily*,
This— I may call him—his adopted fon,
The noble *Tancred*, form'd to all his virtues.

SIGISMUNDA.

Ah form'd to charm his daughter!—This fair morn
Has tempted far the chace.   Is he not yet
Return'd?

LAURA.

   No.—When your father to the king,
Who now expiring lies, was call'd in hafte,

3

He

He fent each way his meffengers to find him ;
With fuch a look of ardour and impatience,
As if this near event was to count *Tancred*
Of more importance than I comprehend.

SIGISMUNDA.

There lies, my *Laura*, o'er my *Tancred*'s birth
A cloud I cannot pierce. With princely accoft,
Nay, with refpect, which oft I have obferv'd,
Stealing at times fubmiffive o'er his features,
In *Belmont*'s woods my father retir'd this youth—
Ah woods ! where firft my artlefs bofom learnt
The fighs of love.—He gives him out the fon
Of an old friend, a baron of *Apulia*,
Who in the late crufade bravely fell.
But then 'tis ftrange; is all his family
As well as father dead ? and all their friends,
Except my fire, the generous good *Siffredi* ?
Had he a mother, fifter, brother left,
The laft remain of kindred ; with what pride,
What rapture, might they fly o'er earth and fea,
To claim this rifing honour of their blood !
This bright unknown ! this all-accomplifh'd youth !
Who charms—too much—the heart of *Sigifmunda !*

   Laura, perhaps your brother knows him better,
The friend and partner of his freeft hours,
What fays *Redolpho ?* Does he truly credit
This ftory of his birth ?

LAURA.

     He has fometimes,

Like

Like you, his doubts ; yet, when maturely weigh'd,
·Believes it true.   As for lord *Tancred*'s felf,
He never entertain'd the flighteft thought
That verg'd to doubt ; but oft laments his ftate,
By cruel fortune fo ill-pair'd to yours.

Sigismunda.

Merit like his, the fortune of the mind,
Beggars all wealth—Then, to your brother, *Laura*,
He talks of me ?

Laura.

Of nothing elfe.   Howe'er
The talk begin, it ends with *Sigifmunda*.
Their morning, noontide, and their evening walks
Are full of you; and all the woods of *Belmont*
Inamour'd with your name——

Sigismunda.

Away, my friend ;
You flatter——yet the dear delufion charms.

Laura.

No *Sigifmunda*, 'tis the ftricteft truth,
Nor half the truth, I tell you.   Even with fondnefs
My brother talks for ever of the paffion,
That fires young *Tancred*'s breaft. So much it ftrikes
      him,
He praifes love as if he were a lover.
He blames the falfe purfuits of vagrant youth,
Calls them gay folly, a miftaken ftruggle
Againft beft-judging Nature.   Heaven, he fays,
In lavifh bounty form'd the heart for love ;

In

In love included all the finer feeds
Of honour, virtue, friendſhip, pureſt bliſs ——

SIGISMUNDA.

Virtuous *Rodolpho !*

LAURA.

Then his pleaſing theme
He varies to the praiſes of your lover——

SIGISMUNDA.

And what, my *Laura,* ſays he on the ſubjeɛt ?

LAURA.

He ſays that, tho' he were not nobly born,
Nature has form'd him noble, generous, brave,
Truly magnanimous, and warmly ſcorning
Whatever bears the ſmalleſt taint of baſeneſs :
That every eaſy virtue is his own ;
Not learnt by painful labour, but inſpir'd,
Implanted in his ſoul—Chiefly one charm
He in his graceful charaɛter obſerves ;
That tho' his paſſions burn with high impatience,
And ſometimes, from a noble heat of nature,
Are ready to fly off ; yet the leaſt check
Of ruling reaſon brings them back to temper,
And gentle ſoftneſs.

SIGISMUNDA.

True ! O true, *Rodolpho !*
Bleſt be thy kindred worth for loving his !
He is all warmth, all amiable fire,
All quick heroic ardor ! temper'd ſoft
With gentleneſs of heart, and manly reaſon !

VOL. IV.   F   If

If Virtue were to wear a human form,
To light it with her dignity and flame,
Then foft'ning mix her fmiles and tender graces;
O. fhe would chufe the perfon of my *Tancred!*
Go on, my friend, go on, and ever praife him;
The fubject knows no bounds, nor can I tire,
While my breaft trembles to that fweeteft mufic!
The heart of woman taftes no truer joy,
Is never flatter'd with fuch dear enchantment——
'Tis more than felfifh vanity—as when
She hears the praifes of the man fhe loves——

LAURA.

Madam, your father comes.

SCENE II.

SIFFREDI, SIGISMUNDA, LAURA.

SIFFREDI.
[To an Attendant as he enters.
Lord Tancred then

Is found?

ATTENDANT.
My lord, he quickly will be here.

I fcarce could keep before him, tho' he bid me
Speed on, to fay he would attend your orders.

SIFFREDI.

'Tis well—retire—You, too, my daughter, leave me.

SIGIS-

SIGISMUNDA.

I go, my father—But how fares the king?

SIFFREDI.

He is no more. Gone to that awful ſtate,
Where kings the crown wear only of their virtues.

SIGISMUNDA.

How bright muſt then be his!—This ſtroke is ſudden.
He was this morning well, when to the chace
Lord *Tancred* went.

SIFFREDI.

'Tis true. But at his years
Death gives ſhort notice—Drooping nature then,
Without a guſt of pain to ſhake it, falls.
His death, my daughter, was that happy period
Which few attain. The duties of his day
Were all diſcharg'd, and gratefully enjoy'd
It's nobleſt bleſſings; calm as evening ſkies,
Was his pure mind, and lighted up with hopes
That open heaven; when, for his laſt long ſleep
Timely prepar'd, a laſſitude of life,
A pleaſing wearineſs of mortal joy,
Fell on his ſoul, and down he ſunk to reſt.
O may my death be ſuch!——He but one wiſh
Left unfulfill'd, which was to ſee count *Tancred*——

SIGISMUNDA.

To ſee count *Tancred!*—Pardon me, my lord——

SIFFREDI.

For what, my daughter?—But, with ſuch emotion,
Why did you ſtart at mention of count *Tancred?*

SIGIS-

SIGISMUNDA.

Nothing—I only hop'd the dying king
Might mean to make some generous just provision
For this your worthy charge, this noble orphan.

SIFFREDI.

And he has done it largely—Leave me now—
I want some private conference with lord *Tancred*.

S C E N E III.

SIFFREDI *alone.*

My doubts are but too true—If these old eyes
Can trace the marks of love, a mutual passion
Has seiz'd, I fear, my daughter and this prince,
My sovereign now—Should it be so? Ah there,
There lurks a brooding tempest, that may shake
My long concerted scheme, to settle firm
The public peace and welfare, which the king
Has made the prudent basis of his will——
Away! unworthy views! you shall not tempt me!
Nor interest, nor ambition shall seduce
My fixt resolve—— perish the selfish thought,
Which our own good prefers to that of millions!—
He comes—my king—unconscious of his fortune.

SCENE IV.

TANCRED, SIFFREDI.

TANCRED.

My lord *Siffredi*, in your looks I read,
Confirm'd, the mournful news that fly abroad
From tongue to tongue—We then, at laft, have loft
The good old king?

SIFFREDI.

Yes, we have loft a father!
The greateft bleffing Heaven beftows on mortals,
And feldom found amidft thefe wilds of time.
A good, a worthy king!—Hear me, my *Tancred*,
And I will tell thee, in a few plain words,
How he deferv'd that beft, that glorious title.
'Tis nought complex, 'tis clear as truth and virtue.
He lov'd his people, deem'd them all his children;
The good exalted, and deprefs'd the bad.
He fpurn'd the flattering crew, with fcorn rejected
Their fmooth advice that only means themfelves,
Their fchemes to aggrandize him into bafenefs:
Nor did he lefs difdain the fecret breath,
The whifper'd tale, that blights a virtuous name.
He fought alone the good of thofe for whom
He was entrufted with the fovereign power:
Well knowing that a people in their rights
And induftry protected; living fafe

Beneath

Beneath the facred fhelter of the laws,
Encourag'd in their genius, arts, and labours,
And happy each as he himfelf deferves,
Are ne'er ungrateful. With unfparing hand
They will for him provide : their filial love
And confidence are his unfailing treafure,
And every honeft man his faithful guard.

TANCRED.

A general face of grief o'erfpreads the city.
I mark'd the people, as I hither came,
In crowds affembled, ftruck with filent forrow,
And pouring forth the nobleft praife of tears.
Thofe whom remembrance of their former woes,
And long experience of the vain illufions
Of youthful hope, had into wife confent
And fear of change correćted, wrung their hands,
And often caſting up their eyes to heaven,
Gave fign of fad conjećture. Others fhew'd,
Athwart their grief, or real or affećted,
A gleam of expećtation, from what chance
And chance might bring. A mingled murmur run
Along the ſtreets ; and, from the lonely court
Of him who can no more affift their fortunes,
I faw the courtier-fry, with eager hafte,
All hurrying to *Conſtantia.*

SIFFREDI.

Noble youth !
I joy to hear from thee thefe juft reflećtions,
Worthy of riper years—But if they feek

Conſtantia,

Conſtantia, truſt me, they miſtake their courſe.

TANCRED.

How! Is ſhe not, my lord, the late king's ſiſter,
Heir to the crown of *Sicily?* the laſt
Of our fam'd *Norman* line, and now our queen?

SIFFREDI.

Tancred, 'tis true; ſhe is the late king's ſiſter,
The ſole ſurviving offspring of that tyrant
William the Bad—ſo for his vices ſtil'd ;
Who ſpilt much noble blood, and ſore oppreſs'd
Th' exhauſted land: whence grievous wars aroſe,
And many a dire convulſion ſhook the ſtate.
When he, whoſe death *Sicilia* mourns to-day,
William, who has and well deſerv'd the name
Of *Good*, ſucceeding to his father's throne,
Reliev'd his country's woes—But to return—
She is the late king's ſiſter, born ſome months
After the tyrant's death, but not next heir.

TANCRED.

You much ſurprise me—May I then preſume
To aſk who is?

SIFFREDI.

Come nearer, noble *Tancred*,
Son of my care! I muſt, on this occaſion,
Conſult thy generous heart; which, when conducted
By rectitude of mind and honeſt virtues,
Gives better counſel than the hoary head—
Then know, there lives a prince, here in *Palermo*,
The lineal offspring of our famous hero,

F 4

Roger

Roger the Firſt.

TANCRED.

Great Heaven!—How far remov'd
From that our mighty founder?

SIFFREDI.

His great grandſon:
Sprung from his eldeſt ſon, who died untimely,
Before his father.

TANCRED.

Ha! the prince you mean
Is he not *Manfred*'s ſon? The generous, brave,
Unhappy *Manfred!* whom the tyrant *William,*
You juſt now mention'd, not content to ſpoil
Of his paternal crown, threw into fetters,
And infamouſly murder'd?

SIFFREDI.

Yes—the ſame.

TANCRED.

By Heavens! I joy to find our *Norman* reign,
The world's ſole light amidſt theſe barbarous ages!
Yet rears its head; and ſhall not, from the lance,
Paſs to the feeble diſtaff—But this prince
Where has he lain conceal'd?

SIFFREDI.

The late good king,
By noble pity mov'd, contriv'd to ſave him
From his dire father's unrelenting rage,
And had him rear'd in private, as became
His birth and hopes, with high and princely nurture.

Till

Till now, too young to rule a troubled ſtate,
By civil broils moſt miſerably torn,
He in his ſafe retreat has lain conceal'd,
His birth and fortune to himſelf unknown ;
But when the dying king to me entruſted,
As to the chancellor of the realm, his will,
His ſucceſſor he nam'd him.

TANCRED.
                    Happy youth !
He then will triumph o'er his father's foes,
O'er haughty *Oſmond*, and the tyrant's daughter.

SIFFREDI.
Ay, that is what I dread—that heat of youth ;
There lurks, I fear, perdition to the ſtate,
I dread the horrors of rekindled war :
Tho' dead, the tyrant ſtill is to be fear'd ;
His daughter's party ſtill is ſtrong, and numerous :
Her friend, earl *Oſmond*, conſtable of *Sicily*,
Experienc'd, brave, high-born, of mighty intereſt.
Better the prince and princeſs ſhould by marriage
Unite their friends, their intereſt and their claims ;
Then will the peace and welfare of the land
On a firm baſis riſe.

TANCRED.
                    My lord *Siffredi*,
If by myſelf I of this prince may judge,
That ſcheme will ſcarce ſucceed—Your prudent age
In vain will counſel, if the heart forbid it—
But wherefore fear ? The right is clearly his ;

F 5   And,

And, under your direction, with each man
Of worth, and stedfast loyalty, to back
At once the king's appointment and his birthright,
There is no ground for fear. They have great odds,
Against th' astonish'd sons of violence,
Who fight with awful justice on their side.
All *Sicily* will rouse, all faithful hearts
Will range themselves around prince *Manfred*'s son.
For me, I here devote me to the service
Of this young prince; I every drop of blood
Will lose with joy, with transport in his cause—
Pardon my warmth—but that, my lord, will never
To this decision come—Then find the prince;
Lose not a moment to awaken in him
The royal soul. Perhaps he now desponding
Pines in a corner, and laments his fortune;
That in the narrower bounds of private life
He must confine his aims, those swelling virtues
Which from his noble father he inherits.

SIFFREDI.

Perhaps, regardless, in the common bane
Of youth he melts, in vanity and love.
But if the seeds of virtue glow within him,
I will awake a higher sense, a love
That grasps the loves and happiness of millions.

TANCRED.

Why that surmise? Or should he love, *Siffredi*,
I doubt not, it is nobly, which will raise
And animate his virtues—O permit me

To

To plead the cause of youth—Their virtue oft
In pleasure's soft enchantment lull'd a while,
Forgets itself; it sleeps and gayly dreams,
Till great occasion rouse it : Then all flame,
It walks abroad, with heighten'd soul and vigour,
And by the change astonishes the world.
Even with a kind of sympathy, I feel
The joy that waits this prince ; when all the powers,
Th' expanding heart can wish, of doing good;
Whatever swells ambition, or exalts
The human soul into divine emotions,
All crowd at once upon him.

SIFFREDI.

Ah, my Tancred,

Nothing so easy as in speculation,
And at a distance seen, the course of honour,
A fair delightful champain strew'd with flowers.
But when the practice comes ; when our fond passions,
Pleasure, and pride, and self-indulgence, throw
Their magic dust around, the prospect roughens :
Then dreadful passes, craggy mountains rise,
Cliffs to be scal'd, and torrents to be stemm'd :
Then toil ensues, and perseverance stern ;
And endless combats with our grosser sense,
Oft lost, and oft renew'd ; and generous pain
For others felt ; and harder lesson still !
Our honest bliss for others sacrific'd ;
And all the rugged task of virtue quails
The stoutest heart of common resolution.

F 6

Few

Few get above this turbid scene of strife.
Few gain the summit, breathe that purest air,
That heavenly ether, which untroubled sees
The storm of vice and passion rage below.

TANCRED.

Most true, my lord. But why thus augure ill?
You seem to doubt this prince. I know him not.
Yet oh, methinks, my heart could answer for him!
The juncture is so high, so strong the gale
That blows from heaven, as thro' the deadest soul
Might breathe the godlike energy of virtue.

SIFFREDI.

Hear him, immortal shades of his great fathers!—
Forgive me, Sir, this trial of your heart:
Thou! Thou art he!

TANCRED.

Siffredi!

SIFFREDI.

Tancred, thou!
Thou art the man, of all the many thousands
That toil upon the bosom of this isle
By Heaven elected to command the rest,
To rule, protect them, and to make them happy!

TANCRED.

Manfred my father! I the last support
Of the fam'd *Norman* line, that awes the world!
I! who this morning wander'd forth an orphan,
Outcast of all but thee, my second father!
Thus call'd to glory! to the first great lot

Of

Of human kind!—O wonder-working Hand
That, in majeſtic ſilence, ſways at will
The mighty movements of unbounded nature ;
O grant me, Heaven! the virtues to ſuſtain
This awful burden of ſo many heroes !
Let me not be exalted into ſhame,
Set up the worthleſs pageant of vain grandeur.

    Meantime I thank the juſtice of the king,
Who has my right bequeath'd me. Thee, *Siffredi*,
I thank thee—O I ne'er enough can thank thee !
Yes, thou haſt been—thou art—ſhalt be my father !
Thou ſhalt direct my unexperienc'd years,
Shalt be the ruling head, and I the hand.

SIFFREDI.

It is enough for me—to ſee my ſovereign
Aſſert his virtues, and maintain his honour.

TANCRED.

I think, my lord, you ſaid the king committed
To you his will. I hope it is not clogg'd
With any baſe conditions, any clauſe,
To tyrannize my heart, and to *Conſtantia*
Enſlave my hand devoted to another.
The hint you juſt now gave of that alliance,
You muſt imagine, wakes my fear. But know,
In this alone I will not bear diſpute,
Not even from thee, *Siffredi !*—Let the council
Be ſtrait aſſembled, and the will there open'd:
Thence iſſue ſpeedy orders to convene,
This day ere noon, the ſenate : where thoſe barons,

Who

Who now are in *Palermo*, will attend,
To pay their ready homage to the king,
Their rightful king, who claims his native crown,
And will not be a king by deeds and parchments.

SIFFREDI.

I go, my liege. But once again permit me
To tell you——Now, now, is the trying crisis,
That must determine of your future reign.
O with heroic rigour watch your heart!
And to the sovereign duties of the king,
Th' unequal'd pleasures of a God on earth,
Submit the common joys, the common passions,
Nay, even the virtues of the private man.

TANCRED.

Of that no more. They not oppose, but aid,
Invigorate, cherish, and reward each other.
The kind all-ruling Wisdom is no tyrant.

SCENE V.

TANCRED *alone.*

Now, generous *Sigismunda*, comes my turn
To shew my love was not of thine unworthy,
When fortune bade me blush to look to thee.
But what is fortune to the wish of love?
A miserable bankrupt! O 'tis poor,
'Tis scanty all, whate'er we can bestow!
The wealth of kings is wretchedness and want!——

Quick,

Quick, let me find her! taſte that higheſt joy,
Th' exalted heart can know, the mixt effuſion
Of gratitude and love!—Behold, ſhe comes!

SCENE VI.

TANCRED, SIGISMUNDA.

TANCRED.

My fluttering ſoul was all on wing to find thee,
My love! my *Sigiſmunda!*

SIGISMUNDA.

   O my *Tancred!*
Tell me, what means this myſtery and gloom
That lowrs around? Juſt now, involv'd in thought,
My father ſhot athwart me—You, my lord,
Seem ſtrangely mov'd—I fear ſome dark event
From the king's death to trouble our repoſe,
That tender calm we in the woods of *Belmont*
So happily enjoy'd——Explain this hurry,
What means it? Say.

TANCRED.

   It means that we are happy!
Beyond our moſt romantic wiſhes happy!

SIGISMUNDA.

You but perplex me more.

      TANCRED.

TANCRED.

It means, my faireſt!
That thou art queen of *Sicily*; and I
The happieſt of mankind! than monarch more!
Becauſe with thee I can adorn my throne.
Manfred, who fell by tyrant *William*'s rage,
Fam'd *Roger*'s lineal iſſue, was my father.

[*Pauſing.*

You droop, my love; dejeçted on a ſudden;
You ſeem to mourn my fortune—The ſoft tear
Springs in thy eye—O let me kiſs it off——
Why this, my *Sigiſmunda*?.

SIGISMUNDA.

Royal *Tancred*,
None at your glorious fortune can like me
Rejoice;—yet me alone, of all *Sicilians*,
It makes unhappy.

TANCRED.

I ſhould hate it then!
Should throw, with ſcorn, the ſplendid ruin from me!—
No, *Sigiſmunda*, 'tis my hope with thee
To ſhare it, whence it draws its richeſt value.

SIGISMUNDA.

You are my ſovereign—I at humble diſtance——

TANCRED.

Thou art my queen! the ſovereign of my ſoul!
You never reign'd with ſuch triumphant luſtre,
Such winning charms as now; yet, thou art ſtill
The dear, the tender, generous *Sigiſmunda!*

Who,

Who, with a heart exalted far above
Thofe felfifh views that charm the common breaft,
Stoop'd from the height of life and courted beauty,
Then, then, to love me, when I feem'd of fortune
The hopelefs outcaft, when I had no friend,
None to protect and own me but thy father.
And would'ft thou claim all goodnefs to thyfelf?
Canft thou thy *Tancred* deem fo dully form'd,
Of fuch grofs clay, juft as I reach the point—
A point my wildeft hopes could never image—
In that great moment, full of every virtue,
That I fhould then fo mean a traitor prove
To the beft blifs and honour of mankind,
So much difgrace the human heart, as then,
For the dead form of flattery and pomp,
The faithlefs joys of courts, to quit kind truth,
The cordial fweets of friendfhip and of love,
The life of life! my all, my *Sigifmunda!*
I could upbraid thy fears, call them unkind,
Cruel, unjuft, an outrage to my heart,
Did they not fpring from love.

                    SIGISMUNDA.
                              Think not, my lord,
That to fuch vulgar doubts I can defcend.
Your heart, I know, difdains the little thought
Of changing with the vain external change
Of circumftance and fortune.   Rather thence
It would, with rifing ardour, greatly feel
A noble pride to fhew itfelf the fame.

                              But,

But, ah! the hearts of kings are not their own.
There is a haughty duty that fubjects them
To chains of ftate, to wed the public welfare,
And not indulge the tender private virtues.
Some high-defcended princefs, who will bring
New power and intereft to your throne, demands
Your royal hand—perhaps *Conftantia*——

TANCRED.

                    She !
O name her not! Were I this moment free,
And difengag'd as he who never felt
The powerful eye of beauty, never figh'd |
For matchlefs worth like thine, I fhould abhor
All thoughts of that alliance.   Her fell father
Moft bafely murder'd mine ; and fhe, his daughter,
Supported by his barbarous party ftill,
His pride inherits, his imperious fpirit,
And infolent pretenfions to my throne.
And canft thou deem me then fo poorly tame,
So cool a traitor to my father's blood,
As from the prudent cowardice of ftate
E'er to fubmit to fuch a bafe propofal ?
Detefted thought ! O doubly, doubly hateful !
From the two ftrongeft paffions ; from averfion
To this *Conftantia*—and from love to thee.
   Cuftom, 'tis true, a venerable tyrant,
O'er fervile man extends her blind dominion :
The pride of kings enflaves them ; their ambition,
Or intereft, lords it o'er the better paffions.
                            But

But vain their talk, mask'd under specious words
Of station, duty, and of public good:
They whom just Heaven has to a throne exalted,
To guard the rights and liberties of others,
What duty binds them to betray their own?
For me, my free-born heart shall bear no dictates,
But those of truth and honour; wear no chains,
But the dear chains of love and *Sigismunda!*
Or if indeed my choice must be directed
By views of public good, whom shall I chuse
So fit to grace, to dignify a crown,
And beam sweet mercy on a happy people,
As thee, my love? whom place upon my throne
But thee, descended from the good *Siffredi!*
'Tis fit that heart be thine, which drew from him
Whate'er can make it worthy thy acceptance.

SIGISMUNDA.

Cease, cease, to raise my hopes above my duty.
Charm me no more, my *Tancred!*—O that we
In those blest woods, where first you won my soul,
Had pass'd our gentle days: far from the toil
And pomp of courts! Such is the wish of love;
Of love, that, with delightful weakness, knows
No bliss and no ambition but itself.
But, in the world's full light, those charming dreams,
Those fond illusions vanish. Awful duties,
The tyranny of men, even your own heart,
Where lurks a sense your passion stifles now,
And proud imperious honour call you from me.

'Tis

'Tis all in vain—You cannot hufh a voice
That murmurs here—I muft not be perfuaded!

TANCRED, kneeling.

Hear me, thou foul of all my hopes and wifhes!
And witnefs, Heaven! prime fource of love and joy!
Not a whole warring world combin'd againft me;
Its pride, its fplendor, its impofing forms,
Nor intereft, nor ambition, nor the face
Of folemn ftate, not even thy father's wifdom,
Shall ever fhake my faith to *Sigifmunda!*

[Trumpets and acclamations heard.

But, hark! the public voice to duties call me,
Which with unweary'd zeal I will difcharge;
And thou, yes thou, fhalt be my bright reward—
Yet—ere I go—to hufh thy lovely fears,
Thy delicate objections———— [*writes his name.*

Take this blank,

Sign'd with my name, and give it to thy father:
Tell him 'tis my command, it be fill'd up,
With a moft ftrict and folemn marriage-contract.
How dear each tie! how charming to my foul!
That more unites me to my *Sigifmunda.*

For thee and for my people's good to live,
Is all the blifs which fovereign power can give.

The End of the Firft Act.

A C T

ACT II. SCENE I.

SIFFREDI *alone.*

SO far 'tis well—The late king's will proceeds
  Upon the plan I counsel'd; that prince *Tancrea*
Shall make *Constantia* partner of his throne.
O great, O wish'd event! whence the dire seeds
Of dark intestine broils, of civil war,
And all its dreadful miseries and crimes,
Shall be for ever rooted from the land.
May these dim eyes, long blasted by the rage
Of cruel faction and my country's woes,
Tir'd with the toils and vanities of life,
Behold this period, then be clos'd in peace!
  But how this mighty obstacle surmount,
Which love has thrown betwixt? Love, that disturbs
The schemes of wisdom still; that, wing'd with passion,
Blind and impetuous in its fond pursuits,
Leaves the grey-headed reason far behind.
Alas! how frail the state of human bliss!
When even our honest passions oft destroy it.
I was to blame, in solitude and shades,

Infectious

Infectious scenes! to trust their youthful hearts.
Would I had mark'd the rising flame! that now
Burns out with dangerous force—My daughter owns
Her passion for the king; she trembling own'd it,
With prayers and tears and tender supplications,
That almost shook my firmness—And this blank,
Which his rash fondness gave her, shews how much,
To what a wild extravagance he loves—
I see no means—it foils my deepest thought—
How to controul this madness of the king,
That wears the face of virtue, and will thence
Disdain restraint, will from his generous heart
Borrow new rage, even speciously oppose
To reason reason—But it must be done.
My own advice, of which I more and more
Approve, the strict conditions of the will,
Highly demand his marriage with *Constantia*;
Or else her party has a fair pretence——
And all, at once, is horror and confusion——
How issue from this maze?—The crowding barons
Here summon'd to the palace, meet already,
To pay their homage, and confirm the will.
On a few moments hangs the public fate,
On a few hasty moments—Ha! there shone
A gleam of hope—Yes—with this very paper
I yet will save him—Necessary means
For good and noble ends can ne'er be wrong.
In that resistless, that peculiar case,
Deceit is truth and virtue—But how hold

2   This

This lion in the toil?—O I will form it
Of such a fatal thread, twist it so strong
With all the ties of honour and of duty,
That his most desperate fury shall not break
The honest snare—Here is the royal hand—
I will beneath it write a perfect, full,
And absolute agreement to the will;
Which read before the nobles of the realm
Assembled, in the sacred face of *Sicily*,
Constantia present, every heart and eye
Fix'd on their monarch, every tongue applauding,
He must submit, his dream of love must vanish—
It shall be done!——To me, I know, 'tis ruin;
But safety to the public, to the king.
I will not reason more, I will not listen
Even to the voice of honour—No—'tis fix'd!
I here devote me for my prince and country;
Let them be safe, and let me nobly perish!

Behold earl *Osmond* comes; without whose aid
My schemes are all in vain.

SCENE II.

Osmond, Siffredi.

Osmond.

My lord *Siffredi*,
I from the council haften'd to *Conftantia*,
And have accomplifh'd what we there propos'd.
The princefs to the will fubmits her claims.
She with her prefence means to grace the fenate,
And of your royal charge young *Tancred*'s hand
Accept. At firft, indeed, it fhock'd her hopes
Of reigning fole, this new furprizing fcene
Of *Manfred*'s fon, appointed by the king
With her joint heir——But I fo fully fhew'd
The juftice of the cafe, the public good
And fure eftablifh'd peace which thence would rife,
Join'd to the ftrong neceffity that urg'd her,
If on *Sicilia*'s throne fhe meant to fit,
As to the wife difpofal of the will
Her high ambition tam'd. Methought, befides,
I could difcern that not from prudence merely
She to this choice fubmitted.

Siffredi.

Noble *Ofmond*,
You have in this done to the public great
And fignal fervice. Yes, I muft avow it;
This frank and ready inftance of your zeal,

3

In fuch a trying crifis of the ftate,
When intereft and ambition might have warp'd
Your views; I own, this truly generous virtue
Upbraids the rafhnefs of my former judgment.

OSMOND.

Siffredi, no.—To you belongs the praife;
The glorious work is yours. Had I not feiz'd,
Improv'd the wifh'd occafion to root out
Divifion from the land, and fave my country,
I had been bafe, been infamous for ever.
'Tis you, my lord, to whom the many thoufands,
That by the barbarous fword of civil war
Had fallen inglorious, owe their lives; to you
The fons of this fair ifle, from her firft peers
Down to the fwain who tills her golden plains,
Owe their fafe homes, their foft domeftic hours,
And thro' late time pofterity fhall blefs you,
You who advis'd this will—I blufh to think,
I have fo long oppos'd the beft good man
In *Sicily*——With what impartial care
Ought we to watch o'er prejudice and paffion,
Nor truft too much the jaundic'd eye of party!
Henceforth its vain delufions I renounce,
Its hot determinations, that confine
All merit and all virtue to itfelf.
To yours I join my hand; with you will own
No intereft and no party but my country.
Nor is your friendfhip only my ambition:
There is a dearer name, the name of father,

By which I fhould rejoice to call *Siffredi*.
Your daughter's hand would to the public weal
Unite my private happinefs.

SIFFREDI.

My lord,
You have my glad confent.   To be allied
To your diftinguifh'd family, and merit,
I fhall efteem an honour.   From my foul
I here embrace earl *Ofmond* as my friend,
And fon.

OSMOND.

You make him happy.   This affent,
So frank and warm, to what I long have wifh'd,
Engages all my gratitude ; at once,
In the firft bloffom, it matures our friendfhip.
I from this moment vow myfelf the friend,
And zealous fervant of *Siffredi*'s houfe.

Enter an Officer belonging to the Court.

OFFICER *to* Siffredi.
The king, my lord, demands your fpeedy prefence.

SIFFREDI.
I will attend him ftrait—Farewel, my lord :
The fenate meets : there, a few moments hence,
I will rejoin you.

OSMOND.

There, my noble lord,
We will complete this falutary work,
Will there begin a new aufpicious era.

7   SCENE

SCENE III.

OSMOND *alone.*

Siffredi gives his daughter to my wifhes—
But does fhe give herfelf? Gay, young, and flatter'd,
Perhaps engag'd, will fhe her youthful heart
Yield to my harfher, uncomplying years?
I am not form'd, by flattery and praife,
By fighs and tears, and all the whining trade
Of love, to feed a fair-one's vanity;
To charm at once and fpoil her. Thefe foft arts
Nor fuit my years nor temper; thefe be left
To boys and doating age. A prudent father,
By nature charg'd to guide and rule her choice,
Refigns his daughter to a hufband's power,
Who with fuperior dignity, with reafon,
And manly tendernefs, will ever love her;
Not firft a kneeling flave, and then a tyrant.

SCENE IV.

OSMOND, BARONS.

OSMOND.

My lords, I greet you well. This wondrous day
Unites us all in amity and friendfhip.
We meet to-day with open hearts and looks,

Not

Not gloom'd by party, fcouling on each other,
But all the children of one happy ifle,
The focial fons of liberty.   No pride,
No paffion now, no thwarting views divide us:
Prince *Manfred*'s line, at laft, to *William*'s join'd,
Combines us in one family of brothers.
This to the late good king's well-order'd will,
And wife *Siffredi*'s generous care we owe.
I truly give you joy.   Firft of you all,
I here renounce thofe errors and divifions
That have fo long difturb'd our peace, and feem'd,
Fermenting ftill, to threaten new commotions—
By time inftructed let us not difdain
To quit miftakes.   We all, my lords, have err'd.
Men may, I find, be honeft, tho' they differ.

ıft BARON.

Who follows not, my lord, the fair example
You fet us all, whate'er be his pretence,
Loves not with-fingle and unbias'd heart
His country as he ought.

2d BARON.

    O beauteous Peace!
Sweet union of a ftate! What elfe, but thou,
Gives fafety, ftrength, and glory to a people!
I bow, lord conftable, beneath the fnow
Of many years; yet in my breaft revives
A youthful flame.   Methinks, I fee again
Thofe gentle days renew'd, that blefs'd our ifle,
Ere by this wafteful fury of divifion,

        Worfe

Worſe than our *Ætna's* moſt deſtructive fires,
It deſolated ſunk. I ſee our plains
Unbounded waving with the gifts of harveſt ;
Our ſeas with commerce throng'd, our buſy ports
With chearful toil. Our *Enna* blooms afreſh ;
Afreſh the ſweets of thymy *Hybla* flow.
Our nymphs and ſhepherds, ſporting in each vale,
Inſpire new ſong, and wake the paſtoral reed—.
The tongue of age is fond—Come, come, my ſons ;
I long to ſee this prince, of whom the world
Speaks largely well—His father was my friend,
The brave unhappy *Manfred*—Come, my lords ;
We tarry here too long.

SCENE V.

Two Officers, *keeping off the Crowd.*

One of the Crowd.

    Shew us our king,
The valiant *Manfred's* ſon, who lov'd the people—
We muſt, we will behold him—Give us way.

1ſt Officer.

Pray, gentlemen, give back—it muſt not be—
Give back, I pray—on ſuch a glad occaſion
I would not ill entreat the loweſt of you.

2d Man *of the Crowd.*

Nay, give us but a glimpſe of our young king.

We

We more than any baron of them all
Will pay him true allegiance.

2d OFFICER.

Friends—indeed—
You cannot pass this way—We have strict orders,
To keep for him himself, and for the barons,
All these apartments clear—Go to the gate
That fronts the sea—You there will find admission.

ALL.

Long live king *Tancred! Manfred*'s son—Huzza!
[*Crowd goes off.*

1st OFFICER.

I do not marvel at their rage of joy:
He is a brave and amiable prince.
When in my lord *Siffredi*'s house I liv'd,
Ere by his favour I obtain'd this office,
I there remember well the young count *Tancred.*
To see him and to love him were the same.
He was so noble in his ways, yet still
So affable and mild—Well, well, old *Sicily,*
Yet happy days await thee !

2d OFFICER.

Grant it, Heaven !
We have seen sad and troublous times enough.
He is, they say, to wed the late king's sister,
Constantia.

1st OFFICER.

Friend, of that I greatly doubt,
Or I mistake, or lord *Siffredi*'s daughter,

The

The gentle *Sigifmunda* has his heart.
If one may judge by kindly cordial looks,
And fond affiduous care to pleafe each other,
Moft certainly they love——O be they bleft,
As they deferve! It were great pity aught
Should part a matchlefs pair : the glory he,
And fhe the blooming grace of *Sicily!*

2d OFFICER.

My lord *Rcdoipho* comes.

SCENE VI.

RODOLPHO, *from the Senate.*

RODOLPHO.

My honeft friends,
You may retire.   [Officers *go out.*
A ftorm is in the wind.
This Will perplexes all.   No, *Tancred* never
Can ftoop to thefe conditions, which at once
Attack his rights, his honour, and his love.
Thofe wife old men, thofe plodding grave ftate pedants,
Forget the courfe of youth ; their crooked prudence,
To bafenefs verging ftill, forgets to take
Into their fine-fpun fchemes the generous heart,
That thro' the cobweb fyftem burfting lays
Their labours wafte—So will this bufinefs prove,
Or I miftake the king—back from the pomp

G 4   He

He feem'd at firft to fhrink ; and round his brow
I mark'd a gathering cloud, when by his fide,
As if defign'd to fhare the public homage,
He faw the tyrant's daughter.   But confefs'd,
At leaft to me, the doubling tempeft frown'd,
And fhook his fwelling bofom, when he heard
Th' unjuft, the bafe conditions of the will.
Uncertain, toft in cruel agitation,
He oft, methought, addrefs d himfelf to fpeak
And interrupt *Siffredi* ; who appear'd,
With confcious hafte, to dread that interruption,
And hurry'd on—but hark ! I hear a noife,
As if th' affembly rofe—Ha ! *Sigifmunda*,
Opprefs'd with grief and wrapt in penfive forrow,
Paffes along——

      [Sigifmunda *and Attendants pafs thro' the
        back fcene.*   Laura *advances.*

S C E N E VII.

RODOLPHO, LAURA.

LAURA.

    Your high-prais'd friend, the king,
Is falfe, moft vilely falfe ! The meaneft flave
Had fhown a nobler heart ; nor grofsly thus,
By the firft bait ambition fpread, been gull'd.
He *Manfred's* fon ! away ! it cannot be !

                   The

The fon of that brave prince could ne'er betray
Thofe rights fo long ufurp'd from his great fathers,
Which he, this day, by fuch amazing fortune,
Had juft regain'd; he ne'er could facrifice
All faith, all honour, gratitude and love,
Even juft refentment of his father's fate,
And pride itfelf; whate'er exalts a man
Above the groveling fons of peafant-mud,
All in a moment—And for what? why truly,
For kind permiffion, gracious leave, to fit
On his own throne with tyrant *William's* daughter!

RODOLPHO.

I ftand amaz'd—You furely wrong him, *Laura.*
There muft be fome miftake.

LAURA.

There can be none!
Siffredi read his full and free confent
Before th' applauding fenate. True indeed,
A fmall remain of fhame, a timorous weaknefs,
Even daftardly in falfhood, made him blufh
To act this fcene in *Sigifmunda's* eye,
Who funk beneath his perfidy and bafenefs.
Hence, till to-morrow he adjourn'd the fenate—
To-morrow fix'd with infamy to crown him!
Then, leading off his gay triumphant princefs,
He left the poor unhappy *Sigifmunda,*
To bend her trembling fteps to that fad home
His faithlefs vows will render hateful to her—
He comes—Farewel—I cannot bear his prefence!

G 5   SCENE

SCENE VIII.

TANCRED, SIFFREDI, RODOLPHO.

TANCRED *entering to* Siffredi.

Avoid me, hoary traitor!—Go, *Rodolpho*,
Give orders that all paſſages this way
Be ſhut—Defend me from a hateful world,
The bane of peace and honour—then return—
  What! doſt thou haunt me ſtill? O monſtrous inſult!
Unparallel'd indignity! Juſt Heaven!
Was ever king, was ever man ſo treated?
So trampled into baſeneſs!

SIFFREDI.

                    Here, my liege,
Here ſtrike! I nor deſerve, nor aſk for mercy.

TANCRED.

Diſtraction!—O my ſoul—Hold, reaſon, hold
Thy giddy ſeat—O this inhuman outrage
Unhinges thought!

SIFFREDI.

          Exterminate thy ſervant!

TANCRED.

All, all but this I could have borne—but this!
This daring inſolence beyond example!
This murderous ſtroke that ſtabs my peace for ever!
That wounds me there—there! where the human heart
Moſt exquiſitely feels——

                              SIFFREDI,

SIFFREDI.

O bear it not,
My royal lord! appeafe on me your vengeance!

TANCRED.

Did ever tyrant image aught fo cruel!
The loweſt ſlave that crawls upon the earth,
Robb'd of each comfort Heaven beſtows on mortals,
On the bare ground, has ſtill his virtue left,
The ſacred treaſures of an honeſt heart,
Which thou haſt dar'd, with raſh audacious hand,
And impious fraud, in me to violate——

SIFFREDI.

Behold, my liege, that raſh audacious hand,
Which not repents its crime—O glorious! happy!
If by my ruin I can ſave your honour.

TANCRED.

Such honour I renounce! with ſovereign ſcorn
Greatly deteſt it, and its mean adviſer!
Haſt thou not dar'd beneath my name to ſhelter—
My name for other purpoſes deſign'd,
Given from the fondneſs of a faithful heart,
With the beſt love o'erflowing—haſt thou not
Beneath thy ſovereign's name baſely preſum'd
To ſhield a lye? a lye! in public utter'd,
To all deluded *Sicily?* But know,
This poor contrivance is as weak as baſe.
In ſuch a wretched toil none can be held
But fools and cowards—Soon thy flimſy arts,
Touch'd by my juſt, my burning indignation,

G 6   Shall

Shall burſt like threads in flame!—Thy doating
    prudence
But more ſecures the purpoſe it would ſhake.
Had my reſolves been wavering and doubtful,
This would confirm them, make them fix'd as fate;
This adds the only motive that was wanting
To urge them on thro' war and deſolation—
What! marry her! *Conſtantia!* Her! the daughter
Of the fell tyrant who deſtroy'd my father!
The very thought is madneſs! Ere thou feeſt
The torch of *Hymen* light theſe hated nuptials,
Thou ſhalt behold *Sicilia* wrapt in flames,
Her cities raz'd, her valleys drench'd with ſlaughter—
Love ſet aſide—my pride aſſumes the quarrel.
My honour now is up; in ſpite of thee,
A world combin'd againſt me, I will give
This ſcatter'd Will in fragments to the winds,
Aſſert my rights, the freedom of my heart,
Cruſh all who dare oppoſe me to the duſt,
And heap perdition on thee!

          SIFFREDI.

               Sir, 'tis juſt.
Exhauſt on me your rage; I claim it all.
But for theſe public threats thy paſſion utters,
'Tis what thou canſt not do!

          TANCRED.

               I cannot! ha!
Driven to the dreadful brink of ſuch diſhonour
Enough to make the tameſt coward brave,

                    And'

SIGISMUNDA.

And into fiercenefs roufe the mildeft nature,
What fhall arreft my vengeance ? who ?

SIFFREDI.

Thyfelf!

TANCRED.

Away ! dare not to juftify thy crime !
That, that alone can aggravate its horror,
Add infolence to infolence—perhaps
May make my rage forget——

SIFFREDI.

O let it burft

On this grey head devoted to thy fervice!
But when the ftorm has vented all its fury,
Thou then muft hear—nay more, I know, thou wilt—
Wilt hear the calm, yet ftronger voice of reafon.
Thou muft reflect that a whole people's fafety,
The weal of trufted millions fhould bear down,
Thyfelf the judge, thy fondeft partial pleafure.
Thou muft reflect that there are other duties,
A nobler pride, a more exalted honour,
Superior pleafures far, that will oblige,
Compel thee, to abide by this my deed,
Unwarranted perhaps in common juftice,
But which Neceffity, even Virtue's tyrant,
With awful voice commanded—Yes, thou muft,
In calmer hours, diveft thee of thy love,
Thefe common paffions of the vulgar breaft,
This boiling heat of youth, and be a king !

The

The lover of thy people !

TANCRED.

Truths ill-employ'd !

Abus'd to colour guilt !—a king ! a king !
Yes, I will be a king. but not a flave !
In this will be a king ! in this my people
Shall learn to judge how I will guard their rights,
When they behold me vindicate my own.
But have I, fay, been treated like a king ?——
Heavens ! could I ftoop to fuch outrageous ufage,
I were a mean, a fhamelefs wretch, unworthy
To wield a fcepter in a land of flaves,
A foil abhorr'd of virtue, fhould belye
My father's blood, belye thofe very maxims,
At other times, you taught my youth—*Siffredi !*

[*In a foften'd tone of voice.*

SIFFREDI.

Behold, my prince, behold thy poor old fervant,
Whofe darling care, thefe twenty years, has been
To nurfe thee up to virtue ; who for thee,
Thy glory and thy weal, renounces all,
All intereft or ambition can pour forth ;
What many a felfifh father would purfue
Thro' treachery and crimes : behold him here,
Bent on his feeble knees, to beg, conjure thee,
With tears to beg thee, to controul thy paffion,
And fave thyfelf, thy honour, and thy people !
Kneeling with me behold the many thoufands

To

To thy protection trusted : Fathers, mothers,
The sacred front of venerable age,
The tender virgin and the helpless infant ;
The ministers of Heaven, those, who maintain,
Around thy throne, the majesty of rule ;
And those, whose labour, scorch'd by winds and sun,
Feeds the rejoicing public : see them all,
Here at thy feet, conjuring thee to save them,
From misery and war, from crimes and rapine !
Can there be aught, kind Heaven! in self-indulgence
To weigh down these ? This aggregate of love,
With which compar'd the dearest private passion
Is but the wasted dust upon the balance ?
Turn not away—Oh is there not some part,
In thy great heart, so sensible to kindness,
And generous warmth, some nobler part, to feel
The prayers and tears of these, the mingled voice
Of Heaven and earth !

TANCRED.

       There is ! and thou hast touch'd it.
Rise, rise, *Siffredi*—Oh ! thou hast undone me,
Unkind old man !—O ill-entreated *Tancred !*
Which way soe'er I turn, dishonour rears
Her hideous front—and misery and ruin !
Was it for this you took such care to form me ?
For this imbued me with the quickest sense
Of shame ; these finer feelings, that ne'er vex
The common mass of mortals, dully happy

                       In

In bleſt inſenſibility ? O rather
You ſhould have fear'd my heart; taught me that power
And ſplendid intereſt lord it ſtill o'er virtue ;
That, gilded by proſperity and pride,
There is no ſhame, no meannefs : temper'd thus,
I had been fit to rule a venal world.
Alas ! what meant thy wantonnefs of prudence ?
Why have you rais'd this miſerable conflict
Betwixt the duties of the king and man ?
Set virtue againſt virtue ?—Ah *Siffredi !*
'Tis thy ſuperfluous, thy unfeeling wiſdom,
That has involv'd me in a maze of error,
Almoſt beyond retreat— But hold, my ſoul,
Thy ſteady purpoſe—Toſt by various paſſions,
To this eternal anchor keep—There is,
Can be no public without private virtue——
Then mark me well, obſerve what I command ;
It is the ſole expedient now remaining—
To-morrow, when the ſenate meets again,
Unfold the whole, unravel the deceit ;
Nor that alone, try to repair its miſchief ;
There all thy power, thy eloquence and intereſt
Exert, to reinſtate me in my rights,
And from thy own dark ſnares to diſembroil me—
Start not, my lord—This muſt and ſhall be done !
Or here, our friendſhip ends—Howe'er diſguis'd,
Whatever thy pretence, thou art a traitor.

SIFFREDI.

SIFFREDI.

I fhould indeed deferve the name of traitor,
And even a traitor's fate, had I fo flightly,
From principles fo weak, done what I did,
As e'er to difavow it——

TANCRED.

Ha!

SIFFREDI.

My liege,
Expect not this—Tho' practis'd long in courts,
I have not fo far learn'd their fubtle trade,
To veer obedient with each guft of paffion.
I honour thee, I venerate thy orders,
But honour more my duty. Nought on earth
Shall ever fhake me from that folid rock,
Nor fmiles nor frowns.——

TANCRED.

You will not then?

SIFFREDI.

I cannot!

TANCRED.

Away! begone!—O my *Rodolpho*, come,
And fave me from this traitor!—Hence, I fay.
Avoid my prefence ftrait! and, know, old man,
Thou my worft foe beneath the mafk of friendfhip,
Who, not content to trample in the duft
My deareft rights, doft with cool infolence
Perfift, and call it duty; hadft thou not

A daughter

A daughter that protects thee, thou shouldst feel
The vengeance thou deservest—No reply!
Away!

S C E N E IX.

TANCRED, RODOLPHO.

RODOLPHO.
What can incense my prince so highly
Against his friend *Siffredi?*

TANCRED.
Friend! *Rodolpho?*
When I have told thee what this friend has done,
How play'd me like a boy, a base-born wretch,
Who had nor heart nor spirit! thou wilt stand
Amaz'd, and wonder at my stupid patience.

RODOLPHO.
I heard, with mixt astonishment and grief,
The king's unjust dishonourable will,
Void in itself—I saw you stung with rage,
And writhing in the snare; just as I went,
At your command, to wait you here—but that
Was the king's deed, not his.

TANCRED.
O he advis'd it!
These many years he has in secret hatch'd
This black contrivance, glories in the scheme,

And

And proudly plumes him with his traiterous virtue.
But that was nought, *Rodolpho*, nothing, nothing!
O that was gentle, blamelefs to what follow'd!
I had, my friend, to *Sigifmunda* given,
To hufh her fears, in the full gufh of fondnefs,
A blank fign'd by my hand—and he, O Heavens!
Was ever fuch a wild attempt!—he wrote
Beneath my name an abfolute compliance
To this detefted Will; nay, dar'd to read it
Before myfelf, on my infulted throne
His idle pageant plac'd—O words are weak
To paint the pangs, the rage, the indignation,
That whirl'd from thought to thought my foul in
       tempeft,
Now on the point to burft, and now by fhame
Reprefs'd—But in the face of *Sicily*,
All mad with acclamation, what, *Rodolpho*,
What could I do? The fole relief that rofe
To my diftracted mind, was to adjourn
Th' affembly till to-morrow—But to-morrow
What can be done?—O it avails not what!
I care not what is done—My only care
Is how to clear my faith to *Sigifmunda*.
She thinks me falfe! She caft a look that kill'd me!
O I am bafe in *Sigifmunda*'s eye!
The loweft of mankind, the moft perfidious!

          RODOLPHO.

This was a ftrain of infolence indeed,
A daring outrage of fo ftrange a nature,
As ftuns me quite——

              TANCRED.

TANCRED.
Curs'd be my timid prudence!
That dash'd not back, that moment in his face,
The bold presumptuous lye—and curs'd this hand!
That from a start of poor dissimulation,
Led off my *Sigismunda*'s hated rival,
Ah then! what poison'd by the false appearance;
What, *Sigismunda*, were thy thoughts of me!
How, in the silent bitterness of soul,
How didst thou scorn me! hate mankind, thyself,
For trusting to the vows of faithless *Tancred* !
For such I seem'd—I was!—The thought distracts me!
I should have cast a flattering world aside,
Rush'd from my throne, before them all avow'd her,
The choice, the glory of my free-born heart,
And spurn'd the shameful fetters thrown upon it—
Instead of that—confusion !——what I did
Has clinch'd the chain, confirm'd *Siffredi*'s crime,
And fix'd me down to infamy!

RODOLPHO.
My lord,
Blame not the conduct, which your situation,
Tore from your tortur'd heart—What could you do?
Had you, so circumstanc'd, in open senate,
Before th' astonish'd public, with no friends
Prepar'd, no party form'd, affronted thus
The haughty princess and her powerful faction,
Supported by this Will, the sudden stroke,
Abrupt and premature, might have recoil'd

Upon

Upon yourſelf, even your own friends revolted,
And turn'd at once the public ſcale againſt you.
Beſides, conſider, had you then detected
In its freſh guilt this action of *Siffredi*,
You muſt with ſignal vengeance have chaſtis'd
The treaſonable deed—Nothing ſo mean
As weak inſulted power that dares not puniſh.
And how would that have ſuited with your love?
His daughter preſent too? Truſt me, your conduct,
Howe'er abhorrent to a heart like yours,
Was fortunate and wiſe—Not that I mean
E'er to adviſe ſubmiſſion——

TANCRED.

                    Heavens! Submiſſion!
Could I deſcend to bear it, even in thought,
Deſpiſe me, you, the world, and *Sigiſmunda!*
Submiſſion!—No!—To-morrow's glorious light
Shall flaſh diſcovery on the ſcene of baſeneſs.
Whatever be the riſque, by Heavens! to morrow,
I will o'erturn the dirty lye-built ſchemes
Of theſe old men, and ſhew my faithful ſenate,
That *Manfred*'s ſon knows to aſſert and wear,
With undiminiſh'd dignity, that crown
This unexpected day has plac'd upon him.

    But this, my friend, theſe ſtormy guſts of pride,
Are foreign to my love—Till *Sigiſmunda*
Be diſabus'd, my breaſt is tumult all,
And can obey no ſettled courſe of reaſon.
I ſee her ſtill, I feel her powerful image,

                                        That

That look, where with reproach complaint was mix'd,
Big with soft woe and gentle indignation,
Which seem'd at once to pity and to scorn me—
O let me find her! I too long have left
My *Sigifmunda* to converfe with tears,
A prey to thoughts that picture me a villain.
But, ah! how, clogg'd with this accurfed ftate,
A tedious world, fhall I now find accefs?
Her father too—Ten thoufand horrors crowd
Into the wild fantaftic eye of love——
Who knows what he may do? Come then, my friend,
And by thy fifter's hand O let me fteal
A letter to her bofom—I no longer
Can bear her abfence, by the juft contempt
She now muft brand me with, inflam'd to madnefs.
Fly, my *Rodolpho*, fly! engage thy fifter
To aid my letter, and this very evening
Secure an interview—I would not bear
This rack another day, not for my kingdom!
Till then deep-plung'd in folitude and fhades,
I will not fee the hated face of man.

Thought drives on thought, on paffions paffions roll;
Her fmiles alone can calm my raging foul.

The End of the Second Act.

ACT III. SCENE I.

SIGISMUNDA *alone, sitting in a disconsolate posture.*

AH tyrant prince! ah more than faithless *Tancred!*
  Ungenerous and inhuman in thy falshood!
Hadst thou, this morning, when my hopeless heart,
Submissive to my fortune and my duty,
Had so much spirit left, as to be willing
To give thee back thy vows, ah! hadst thou then
Confess'd the sad, necessity thy state
Impos'd upon thee, and with gentle friendship,
Since we must part at last, our parting soften'd;
I should indeed—I should have been unhappy,
But not to this extreme—Amidst my grief,
I had, with pensive pleasure, cherish'd still
The sweet remembrance of thy former love,
Thy image still had dwelt upon my soul,
And made our guiltless woes not undelightful.
But coolly thus—How couldst thou be so cruel?—
Thus to revive my hopes, to soothe my love
And call forth all its tenderness, then sink me
In black despair—What unrelenting pride

Possess'd

Possess'd thy breast, that thou couldst bear unmov'd
To see me bent beneath a weight of shame?
Pangs thou canst never feel! How couldst thou drag me
In barbarous triumph at a rival's car?
How make me witness to a fight of horror?
That hand, which, but a few short hours ago,
So wantonly abus'd my simple faith,
Before th' attesting world given to another,
Irrevocably given!—There was a time,
When the least cloud that hung upon my brow,
Perhaps imagin'd only, touch'd thy pity.
Then, brighten'd often by the ready tear,
Thy looks were softness all; then the quick heart,
In every nerve alive, forgot itself,
And for each other then we felt alone.
But now, alas! those tender days are fled;
Now thou canst see me wretched, pierc'd with anguish,
With studied anguish of thy own creating,
Nor wet thy harden'd eye—Hold, let me think—
I wrong thee sure; thou canst not be so base,
As meanly in my misery to triumph——
What is it then?—Why should I search for pain?—
O, 'tis as bad!—'Tis ficklenefs of nature,
'Tis sickly love extinguish'd by ambition——
Is there, kind Heaven! no constancy in man?
No stedfast truth, no generous fix'd affection,
That can bear up against a selfish world?
No, there is none—Even *Tancred* is inconstant!

[*Rising.*
Hence!

Hence! let me fly this scene!—Whate'er I see,
These roofs, these walls, each object that surrounds me,
Are tainted with his vows—But whither fly?
The groves are worse, the soft retreat of *Belmont*,
Its deepening glooms, gay lawns, and airy summits,
Will wound my busy memory to torture,
And all its shades will whisper—faithless *Tancred!*—
My father comes—How, sunk in this disorder,
Shall I sustain his presence?

SCENE II.

SIFFREDI, SIGISMUNDA.

SIFFREDI.
Sigismunda,
My dearest child! I grieve to find thee thus
A prey to tears. I know the powerful cause
From which they flow, and therefore can excuse them,
But not their wilful obstinate continuance.
Come, rouse thee then, call up thy drooping spirit,
Come, wake to reason from this dream of love,
And shew the world thou art *Siffredi*'s daughter.

SIGISMUNDA.
Alas! I am unworthy of that name.

SIFFREDI.
Thou art indeed to blame; thou hast too rashly

Engag'd thy heart, without a father's fanction.
But this I can forgive. The king has virtues,
That plead thy full excuse; nor was I void
Of blame, to truft thee to thofe dangerous virtues.
Then dread not my reproaches. Tho' he blames,
Thy tender father pities more than blames thee.
Thou art my daughter ftill; and, if thy heart
Will now refume its pride, affert itfelf,
And greatly rife fuperior to this trial,
I to my warmeft confidence again
Will take thee, and efteem thee more my daughter.

SIGISMUNDA.

O you are gentler far than I deferve!
It is, it ever was, my darling pride,
To bend my foul to your fupreme commands,
Your wifeft will; and tho' by love betray'd—
Alas! and punifh'd too--I have tranfgrefs'd
The niceft bounds of duty, yet I feel
A fentiment of tendernefs, a fource
Of filial nature fpringing in my breaft,
That fhould it kill me, fhall controul this paffion,
And make me all fubmiffion and obedience
To you my honoured lord, the beft of fathers.

SIFFREDI.

Come to my arms, thou comfort of my age!
Thou only joy and hope of thefe grey hairs!
Come! let me take thee to a parent's heart;
There, with the kindly aid of my advice,
Even with the dew of thefe paternal tears,

2   Revive

Revive and nourifh this becoming fpirit ——
Then thou doft promife me, my *Sigifmunda*——
Thy father ftoops to make it his requeft——
Thou wilt refign thy fond prefumptuous hopes,
And henceforth never more indulge one thought
That in the light of love regards the king ?

SIGISMUNDA.

Hopes I have none !—Thofe by this fatal day
Are blafted all—But from my foul to banifh
While weeping memory there retains her feat,
Thoughts which the pureft bofom might have cherifh'd,
Once my delight, now even in anguifh charming,
Is more, alas ! my lord, than I can promife.

SIFFREDI.

Abfence and time, the foftener of our paffions,
Will conquer this.   Mean time, I hope from thee
A generous great effort ; that thou wilt now
Exert thy utmoft force, nor languifh thus
Beneath the vain extravagance of love.
Let not thy father blufh to hear it faid,
His daughter was fo weak, e'er to admit
A thought fo void of reafon, that a king
Should to his rank, his honour and his glory,
The high important duties of a throne,
Even to his throne itfelf, madly prefer
A wild romantic paffion, the fond child
Of youthful dreaming thought and vacant hours;
That he fhould quit his heaven-appointed ftation,
Defert his aweful charge, the care of all

The

The toiling millions which this ifle contains ;
Nay more, fhould plunge them into war and ruin :
And all to foothe a fick imagination,
A miferable weaknefs—Muft for thee,
To make thee bleft, *Sicilia* be unhappy ?
The king himfelf, loft to the nobler fenfe
Of manly praife, become the piteous heroe
Of fome foft tale, and rufh on fure deftruction ?
Canft thou, my daughter, let the monftrous thought
Poffefs one moment thy perverted fancy ?
Roufe thee, for fhame ! and if a fpark of virtue
Lies flumbering in thy foul, bid it blaze forth ;
Nor fink unequal to the glorious leffon,
This day thy lover gave thee from his throne.

SIGISMUNDA.

Ah ! that was not from virtue !—Had, my father,
That been his aim, I yield to what you fay ;
'Tis powerful truth, unanfwerable reafon.
Then, then, with fad but duteous refignation,
I had fubmitted as became your daughter ;
But in that moment, when my humbled hopes
Were to my duty reconcil'd, to raife them
To yet a fonder height than e'er they knew,
Then rudely dafh them down—There is the fting !
The blafting view is ever prefent to me——
Why did you drag me to a fight fo cruel ?

SIFFREDI.

It was a fcene to fire thy emulation.

SIGISMUNDA.

It was a scene of perfidy !—But know,
I will do more than imitate the king—
For he is falfe !—I, tho' fincerely pierc'd
With the beft, trueft paffion, ever touch'd
A virgin's breaft, here vow to Heaven and you,
Tho' from my heart I cannot, from my hopes
To caft this prince—What would you more, my father?

SIFFREDI.

Yes, one thing more—thy father then is happy—
   Tho' by the voice of innocence and virtue
Abfolv'd, we live not to ourfelves alone :
A rigorous world, with peremptory fway,
Subjects us all, and even the nobleft moft.
This world from thee, my honour and thy own,
Demands one ftep; a ftep, by which convinc d
The king may fee thy heart difdains to wear
A chain which his has greatly thrown afide,
'Tis fitting too, thy fex's pride commands thee,
To fhew th' approving world thou can'ft refign,
As well as he, nor with inferior fpirit,
A paffion fatal to the public weal.
But above all, thou muft root out for ever
From the king's breaft the leaft remain of hope,
And henceforth make his mentioned love difhonour.
Thefe things, my daughter, that muft needs be done,
Can but this way be done—by the fafe refuge,
The facred fhelter of a hufband's arms.
And there is one—

SIGISMUNDA.
Good Heavens! what means my lord?
SIFFREDI.
One of illuftrious family, high rank
Yet ftill of higher dignity and merit,
Who can and will proteɕt thee ; one to awe
The king himfelf—Nay, hear me, *Sigifmunda*—
The noble *Ofmond* courts thee for his bride,
And has my plighted word—This day—

SIGISMUNDA *kneeling*.
My father!
Let me with trembling arms embrace thy knees!
O if you ever wifh to fee me happy ;
If e'er in infant years I gave you joy,
When, as I prattling twin'd around your neck,
You fnatch'd me to your bofom, kifs'd my eyes,
And melting faid you faw my mother there ;
O fave me from that worft feverity
Of fate! O outrage not my breaking heart
To that degree !—I cannot !—'tis impoffible !—
So foon withdraw it, give it to another—
Hear me, my deareft father ! hear the voice
Of nature and humanity, that plead
As well as juftice for me !—Not to chufe
Without your wife direɕtion may be duty ;
But ftill my choice is free—That is a right,
Which even the loweft flave can never lofe.
And would you thus degrade me? make me bafe?
For fuch it were to give my worthlefs perfon
Without

Without my heart, an injury to *Osmond*,
The higheſt can be done—Let me, my lord—
Or I ſhall die, ſhall by the ſudden change
Be to diſtraction ſhock'd—Let me wear out
My hapleſs days in ſolitude and ſilence,
Far from the malice of a prying world!
At leaſt—you cannot ſure refuſe me this——
Give me a little time—I will do all,
All I can do, to pleaſe you!—O your eye
Sheds a kind beam——

SIFFREDI.

My daughter! you abuſe
The ſoftneſs of my nature—

SIGISMUNDA.

Here, my father,
Till you relent, here will I grow for ever!

SIFFREDI.

Riſe, *Sigiſmunda*.—Tho' you touch my heart,
Nothing can ſhake th' inexorable dictates
Of honour, duty, and determin'd reaſon.
Then by the holy ties of filial love,
Reſolve, I charge thee, to receive earl *Osmond*,
As ſuits the man who is thy father's choice,
And worthy of thy hand—I go to bring him—

SIGISMUNDA.

Spare me, my deareſt father!

SIFFREDI, *aſide*.

I muſt ruſh
From her ſoft graſp, or nature will betray me!

H 4   O grant

O grant us, Heaven! that fortitude of mind,
Which liftens to our duty, not our paffions—
   Quit me, my child!

         SIGISMUNDA.

           You cannot, O my father!
You cannot leave me thus!

         SIFFREDI.

           Come hither, *Laura,*
Come to thy friend. Now fhew thyfelf a friend.
Combat her weaknefs; diffipate her tears;
Cherifh, and reconcile her to her duty.

S C E N E III.

SIGISMUNDA, LAURA.

         SIGISMUNDA.

O woe on woe! diftreft by love and duty!
O every way unhappy *Sigifmunda!*

         LAURA.

Forgive me, Madam, if I blame your grief.
How can you wafte your tears on one fo falfe?
Unworthy of your tendernefs? to whom
Nought but contempt is due and indignation?

         SIGISMUNDA.

You know not half the horrors of my fate!
I might perhaps have learn'd to fcorn his falfhood;
Nay, when the firft fad burft of tears was paft,

                  I might

I might have rous'd my pride and fcorn'd himfelf—
But 'tis too much, this greateft laft misfortune—
O whither fhall I fly? Where hide me, *Laura*,
From the dire fcene my father now prepares!

LAURA.

What thus alarms you, Madam?

SIGISMUNDA.

Can it be?
Can I——ah no!——at once give to another
My violated heart? in one wild moment?
He brings earl *Ofmond* to receive my vows!
O dreadful change! for *Tancred* haughty *Ofmond!*

LAURA.

Now, on my foul, 'tis what an outrag'd heart
Like yours, fhould wifh!—I fhould, by Heavens,
efteem it
Moft exquifite revenge!

SIGISMUNDA.

Revenge on whom?
On my own heart, already but too wretched!

LAURA.

On him! this *Tancred!* who has bafely fold,
For the dull form of defpicable grandeur,
His faith, his love!—At once a flave and tyrant!

SIGISMUNDA.

O rail at me, at my believing folly,
My vain ill-founded hopes, but fpare him, *Laura!*

LAURA.

Who rais'd thefe hopes? who triumphs o'er that
weaknefs?

H 5   Pardon

Pardon the word—You greatly merit him ;
Better than him, with all his giddy pomp !
You rais'd him by your fmiles when he was nothing !
Where is your woman's pride ? that guardian fpirit
Given us to dafh the perfidy of man ?
Ye Powers ! I cannot bear the thought with patience—
Yet recent from the moft unfparing vows
The tongue of love e'er lavifh'd ; from your hopes
So vainly, idly, cruelly deluded ;
Before the public thus, before your father,
By an irrevocable folemn deed,
With fuch inhuman fcorn, to throw you from him !
To give his faithlefs hand yet warm from thine,
With complicated meannefs, to *Conftantia !*
And to complete his crime, when thy weak limbs
Could fcarce fupport thee, then, of thee regardlefs,
To lead her off !

SIGISMUNDA.

That was indeed a fight
To poifon love ! to turn it into rage
And keen contempt !—What means this ftupid
weaknefs
That hangs upon me ? Hence unworthy tears !
Difgrace my cheek no more ! No more, my heart,
For one fo coolly falfe or meanly fickle ——
O it imports not which—dare to fuggeft
The leaft excufe !—Yes, traitor, I will wring
Thy pride, will turn thy triumph to confufion !
I will not pine away my days for thee,

Sighing

Sighing to brooks and groves; while, with vain pity,
You in a rival's arms lament my fate——
No! let me perish! ere I tamely be
That foft, that patient, gentle *Sigifmunda*,
Who can confole her with the wretched boaft,
She was for thee unhappy!——If I am,
I will be nobly fo!——*Sicilia*'s daughters
Shall wondering fee in me a great example
Of one who punifh'd an ill-judging heart,
Who made it bow to what it moft abhorr'd!
Crufh'd it to mifery! for having thus
So lightly liften'd to a worthlefs lover!

LAURA.

At laft it mounts! the kindling pride of virtue!
Truft me, thy marriage will embitter his——

SIGISMUNDA.

O may the furies light his nuptial torch!
Be it accurs'd as mine! for the fair peace,
The tender joys of hymeneal love,
May jealoufy awak'd, and fell remorfe,
Pour all their fierceft venom thro' his breaft!——
Where the Fates lead, and blind revenge, I follow!——
Let me not think—By injur'd love I vow,
Thou fhalt, bafe prince perfidious and inhuman!
Thou fhalt behold me in another's arms
In his thou hateft! *Ofmond*'s

LAURA.

                    That will wound

His heart with fecret rage! Ay, t
H 6

His foul to madnefs! fet him up a terror,
A fpectacle of woe to faithlefs lovers! ——
Your cooler thought, befides, will of the change
Approve, and think it happy. Noble *Ofmond*
From the fame ftock with him derives his birth,
Firft of *Sicilian* barons, prudent, brave,
Of ftricteft honour, and by all rever'd——

SIGISMUNDA.

Talk not of *Ofmond*, but perfidious *Tancred!*
Rail at him, rail! invent new names of fcorn!
Affift me, *Laura*; lend my rage frefh fuel;
Support my ftaggering purpofe, which already
Begins to fail me—Ah, my vaunts how vain!
How have I ly'd to my own heart!—Alas!
My tears return, the mighty flood o'erwhelms me!
Ten thoufand crowding images diftract
My tortur'd thought——And is it come to this?
Our hopes? our vows? our oft repeated wifhes,
Breath'd from the fervent foul, and full of heaven,
To make each other happy?—come to this!

LAURA.

If thy own peace and honour cannot keep
Thy refolution fix'd, yet, Sigifmunda,
O think, how deeply, how beyond retreat,
Thy father is engag'd.

SIGISMUNDA.

Ah wretched weaknefs!
That thus enthrals my foul, that chafes thence
Each nobler thought, the fenfe of every duty!—

And

And have I then no tears for thee, my father?
Can I forget thy cares, from helpless years,
Thy tendernefs for me? an eye ftill beam'd
With love? a brow that never knew a frown?
Nor a harfh word thy tongue? Shall I for thefe
Repay thy ftooping venerable age,
With fhame, difquiet, anguifh, and difhonour?
It muft not be!—Thou firft of angels! come,
Sweet filial Piety! and firm my breaft!
Yes, let one daughter to her fate fubmit.
Be nobly wretched—but her father happy!——
Laura!—they come!—O Heavens! I cannot ftand
The horrid trial!—Open, open earth!
And hide me from their view!

LAURA.

Madam!

SCENE IV.

SIFFREDI, OSMOND, SIGISMUNDA, LAURA.

SIFFREDI.

My daughter,
Behold my noble friend who courts thy hand,
And whom to call my fon I fhall be proud;
Nor fhall I lefs be pleas'd in his alliance,
To fee thee happy.

OSMOND,

OSMOND.

Think not, I prefume,
Madam, on this your father's kind confent,
To make me bleft.   I love you from a heart,
That feeks your good fuperior to my own ;
And will, by every art of tender friendfhip,
Confult your deareft welfare.   May I hope,
Yours does not difavow your father's choice ?

SIGISMUNDA.

I am a daughter, Sir—and have no power
O'er my own heart—I die—Support me, *Laura*.

[*Faints.*

SIFFREDI.

Help—Bear her off—She breathes—my daughter !—

SIGISMUNDA.

Oh !—

Forgive my weaknefs—foft—my *Laura*, lead me—
To my apartment.

SIFFREDI.

Pardon me, my lord,
If by this fudden accident alarm'd,
I leave you for a moment.

SCENE

SCENE V.

OSMOND *alone.*

Let me think——
What can this mean?——Is it to me averſion?
Or is it, as I fear'd, ſhe loves another?
Ha!—yes—perhaps the king, the young count
  Tancred!
They were bred up together——Surely that,
That cannot be—Has he not given his hand,
In the moſt ſolemn manner, to *Conſtantia?*
Does not his crown depend upon the deed?
No—if they lov'd, and this old ſtateſman knew it,
He could not to a king prefer a ſubject.
His virtues I eſteem—nay more; I truſt them——
So far as virtue goes—but could he place
His daughter on the throne of *Sicily*——
O 'tis a glorious bribe, too much for man!——
What is it then?—I care not what it be.
My honour now, my dignity demands,
That my propos'd alliance, by her father,
And even herſelf accepted, be not ſcorn'd.
I love her too—I never knew till now
To what a pitch I lov'd her. O ſhe ſhot
Ten thouſand charms into my inmoſt ſoul!
She look'd ſo mild, ſo amiably gentle,
See bow'd her head, ſhe glow'd with ſuch confuſion,
Such lovelineſs of modeſty! She is,

        In

In gracious mind, in manners, and in perfon,
The perfect model of all female beauty!—
She muft be mine—She is!—If yet her heart
Confents not to my happinefs, her duty,
Join'd to my tender cares, will gain fo much
Upon her generous nature—That will follow.

  The man of fenfe, who acts a prudent part,
Not flattering fteals, but forms himfelf the heart.

The End of the Third Act.

ACT IV. SCENE I.

The Garden belonging to SIFFREDI'*s House.*

SIGISMUNDA, LAURA,

SIGISMUNDA, *with a letter in her hand.*

'TIS done!—I am a flave!—The fatal vow
Has pafs'd my lips!—Methought in thofe
fad moments,
The tombs around, the faints, the darken'd altar,
And all the trembling fhrines with horror fhook.
But here is ftill new matter of diftrefs.
O *Tancred* ceafe to perfecute me more!
O grudge me not fome calmer ftate of woe!
Some quiet gloom to fhade my hopelefs days,
Where I may never hear of love and thee!——
Has *Laura* too confpir'd againft my peace?
Why did you take this letter?—bear it back—
                    [*Giving her the letter.*
I will not court new pain.
                    LAURA.
                    Madam, *Rodolpho*
                                   Urg'd

Urg'd me fo much, nay, even with tears conjur'd me,
But this once more to ferve th' unhappy king—
For fuch he faid he was—that tho' enrag'd,
Equal with thee, at his inhuman falfhood,
I could not to my brother's fervent prayers
Refufe this office—Read it—His excufes
Will only more expofe his falfhood.

SIGISMUNDA.

                              No.
It fuits not *Ofmond*'s wife to read one line
From that contagious hand—fhe knows too well!

LAURA.

He paints him out diftrefs'd beyond expreffion,
Even on the point of madnefs. Wild as winds,
And fighting feas, he raves. His paffions mix,
With ceafelefs rage, all in each giddy moment.
He dies to fee you and to clear his faith.

SIGISMUNDA.

Save me from that!—That would be worfe than all!

LAURA.

I but **report my brother's words**; who then
Began to talk of fome dark impofition,
That had deceiv'd us all: when, interrupted,
We heard your father and earl *Ofmond* near,
As fummon'd to *Conftantia*'s court they went.

SIGISMUNDA.

Ha! impofition?—Well! If I am doom'd
To be, o'er all my fex, the wretch of love,
In vain I would refift—Give me the letter—

                                        To

To know the worſt is ſome relief——Alas!
It was not thus, with ſuch dire palpitations,
That, *Tancred*, once I us'd to read thy letters.

[Attempting to read the letter, but gives it to Laura.
Ah fond remembrance blinds me!—Read it, *Laura*.

LAURA *reads*.

Deliver me, Sigiſmunda, *from that moſt exquiſite miſery which a faithful heart can ſuffer—To be thought baſe by her, from whoſe eſteem even virtue borrows new charms. When I ſubmitted to my cruel ſituation, it was not falſhood you beheld, but an exceſs of love. Rather than endanger that, I for a while gave up my honour. Every moment till I ſee you ſtabs me with ſeverer pangs than real guilt itſelf can feel. Let me then conjure you to meet me in the garden, towards the cloſe of the day, when I will explain this myſtery. We have been moſt inhumanly abuſed; and that by the means of the very paper which I gave you, from the warmeſt ſincerity of love, to aſſure to you the heart and hand of*

Tancred.

SIGISMUNDA.

There, *Laura*, there, the dreadful ſecret ſprung!
That paper! ah that paper! it ſuggeſts
A thouſand horrid thoughts—I to my father
Gave it; and he perhaps—I dare not caſt
A look that way—If yet indeed you love me,
O blaſt me not, kind *Tancred* with the truth!
O pitying keep me ignorant for ever!
What ſtrange peculiar miſery is mine?

Reduc'd

Reduc'd to wifh the man I love were falfe?
Why was I hurry'd to a ftep fo rafh?
Repairlefs woe!—I might have waited, fure,
A few fhort hours—No duty that forbade—
I ow'd thy love that juftice; till this day
Thy love an image of all-perfect goodnefs!
A beam from Heaven that glow'd with every virtue!
And have I thrown this prize of life away?
The piteous wreck of one diftracted moment?
Ah the cold prudence of remorfelefs age!
Ah parents, traitors to your children's blifs!
Ah curs'd, ah blind revenge!—On every hand
I was betray'd—You, *Laura*, too, betray'd me!—

LAURA.

Who, who, but he, whate'er he writes, betray'd you?
Or falfe or pufillanimous.. For once,
I will with you fuppofe, that his agreement
To the king's will was forg'd—Tho' forg'd by whom?
Your father fcorns the crime—Yet what avails it?
This, if it clears his truth, condemns his fpirit.
A youthful king, by love and honour fir'd,
Patient to fit on his infulted throne,
And let an outrage, of fo high a nature,
Unpunifh'd pafs, unchcck'd, uncontradicted—
O 'tis a meannefs equal even to falfhood.

SIGISMUNDA.

Laura, no more—We have already judg'd
Too largely without knowledge. Oft, what feems
A trifle, a meer nothing, by itfelf,

In

In some nice situations, turns the scale
Of Fate, and rules the most important actions.
Yes, I begin to feel a sad presage:
I am undone, from that eternal source
Of human woes—The judgment of the passions.
But what have I to do with these excuses?
O cease my treacherous heart to give them room!
It suits not thee to plead a lover's cause;
Even to lament my fate is now dishonour.
Nought now remains, but with relentless purpose,
To shun all interviews, all clearing up
Of this dark scene; to wrap myself in gloom,
In solitude and shades; there to devour
The silent sorrows ever swelling here;
And since I must be wretched—for I must——
To claim the mighty misery myself,
Engross it all, and spare a hapless father.
Hence, let me fly!—the hour approaches——

LAURA.

Madam,

Behold he comes—the king—

SIGISMUNDA.

Heavens! how escape?

No—I will stay—This one last meeting—Leave me.

SCENE II.

TANCRED, SIGISMUNDA.

TANCRED.

And are thefe long long hours of torture paft?
My life! my *Sigifmunda!*

[*Throwing himfelf at her feet.*

SIGISMUNDA.

Rife, my lord.

To fee my fovereign thus no more becomes me.

TANCRED.

O let me kifs the ground on which you tread!
Let me exhale my foul in fofteft tranfport!
Since I again embrace my *Sigifmunda!* [*Rifing.*

Unkind! how couldft thou ever deem me falfe?
How thus difhonour love?—O I could much
Embitter my complaint!—How low were then
Thy thoughts of me? How didft thou then affront
The human heart itfelf? After the vows,
The fervent truth, the tender proteftations,
Which mine has often pour'd, to let thy breaft,
Whate'er th' appearance was, admit fufpicion?

SIGISMUNDA.

How! when I heard myfelf your full confent
To the late king's fo juft and prudent will?
Heard it before you read, in folemn fenate?

When

When I beheld you give your royal hand,
To her, whofe birth and dignity of right,
Demands that high alliance? Yes, my lord,
You have done well. The man, whom Heaven ap-
     points
To govern others, fhould himfelf firft learn
To bend his paffions to the fway of reafon.
In all you have done well; but when you bid
My humbled hopes look up to you again,
And footh'd with wanton cruelty my weaknefs—
That too was well—My vanity deferv'd
The fharp rebuke, whofe fond extravagance
Could ever dream to balance your repofe,
Your glory and the welfare of a people.

TANCRED.

Chide on, chide on. Thy foft reproaches now
Inftead of wounding, only foothe my fondnefs.
No, no, thou charming confort of my foul!
I never lov'd thee with fuch faithful ardour,
As in that cruel miferable moment
You thought me falfe; when even my honour ftoop'd
To wear for thee a baffled face of bafenefs.
It was thy barbarous father, *Sigifmunda,*
Who caught me in the toil. He turn'd that paper,
Meant for th' affuring bond of nuptial love,
To ruin it for ever; he, he wrote
That forg'd confent, you heard, beneath my name,
Nay dar'd before my out-rag'd throne to read it!
Had he not been thy father—Ha! my love!
You tremble, you grow pale.

SIGIS-

SIGISMUNDA.

   Oh leave me, *Tancred!*

TANCRED.

No!—Leave thee?—Never! never! till you set
My heart at peace, till thefe dear lips again
Pronounce thee mine! Without thee I renounce
Myfelf, my friends, the world—Here on this hand—

SIGISMUNDA.

My lord, forget that hand, which never now
Can be to thine united——

TANCRED.

   Sigifmunda!

What doft thou mean?—Thy words, thy look, thy
   manner,
Seem to conceal fome horrid fecret—Heavens!——
No—That was wild—Diftraction fires the thought!—

SIGISMUNDA.

Enquire no more——I never can be thine.

TANCRED.

What, who fhall interpofe? who dares attempt
To brave the fury of an injur'd king?
Who, ere he fees thee ravifh'd from his hopes,
Will wrap all blazing *Sicily* in flames—

SIGISMUNDA.

In vain your power, my lord—This fatal error,
Join'd to my father's unrelenting will,
Has plac'd an everlafting bar betwixt us—
I am—earl *Ofmond's*—Wife.

TANCRED.

Earl *Osmond*'s wife!——

[*After a long pause, during which they
look at one another with the highest
agitation and most tender distress.*

Heavens! did I hear thee right? what! marry'd?
marry'd!

Lost to thy faithful *Tancred!* lost for ever!

Couldst thou then doom me to such matchless woe,

Without so much as hearing me?—Distraction!—

Alas! what hast thou done? Ah *Sigismunda!*—

Thy rash credulity has done a deed,

Which of two happiest lovers—that e'er felt

The blissful power, has made two finish'd wretches!

But—Madness!——Sure, thou know'st it cannot be!

This hand is mine! a thousand thousand vows——

S C E N E III.

TANCRED, OSMOND, SIGISMUNDA.

OSMOND.

[*Snatching her hand from the king.*

Madam, this hand, by the most solemn rites,

A little hour ago, was given to me,

And did not sovereign honour now command me,

Never but with my life to quit my claim,

I would renounce it——thus!

TANCRED.

Ha! who art thou?
Presumptuous man!

SIGISMUNDA, *aside.*

Where is my father? Heavens!

[*Goes out.*

OSMOND.

One thou shouldst better know—Yes—view me—one!
Who can and will maintain his rights and honour,
Against a faithless prince, an upstart king,
Whose first base deed is what a harden'd tyrant
Would blush to act.

TANCRED.

Infolent *Osmond!* know,
This upstart king will hurl confusion on thee,
And all who shall invade his sacred rights,
Prior to thine—Thine founded on compulsion,
On infamous deceit, while his proceed
From mutual love and free long-plighted faith.
She is, and shall be mine!—I will annul,
By the high power with which the laws invest me,
Those guilty forms in which you have entrap'd,
Basely entrap'd, to thy detested nuptials,
My queen betroth'd; who has my heart, my hand,
And shall partake my throne—If, haughty lord,
If this thou didst not know, then know it now!
And know besides, as I have told thee this,
Shouldst thou but think to urge thy treason further—
Than treason more! Treason against my love!——

Thy

Thy life ſhall anſwer for it !

OSMOND.

Ha ! my life !———

It moves my ſcorn to hear thy empty threats.
When was it that a *Norman* baron's life
Became ſo vile, as on the frown of kings
To hang ?—Of that, my lord, the law muſt judge:
Or if the law be weak, my guardian ſword—

TANCRED.

Dare not to touch it, traitor ! leſt my rage
Break looſe, and do a deed that miſbecomes me.

S C E N E IV.

TANCRED, SIFFREDI, OSMOND.

SIFFREDI *entering.*

My gracious lord ! what is it I behold !
My ſovereign in contention with his ſubjects ?
Surely this houſe deſerves from royal *Tancred*
A little more regard, than to be made
A ſcene of trouble and unſeemly jars.
It grieves my ſoul, it baffies every hope,
It makes me ſick of life, to ſee thy glory
Thus blaſted in the bud —Heavens ! can your highneſs
From your exalted character deſcend,
The dignity of virtue ; and, inſtead
Of being the protector of our rights,

I 2   The

The holy guardian of domeftic blifs,
Unkindly thus difturb the fweet repofe,
The fecret peace of families, for which
Alone the freeborn race of man to laws
And government fubmitted ?

TANCRED.

My lord *Siffredi*,
Spare thy rebuke. The duties of my ftation
Are not to me unknown.—But thou, old man,
Doft thou not blufh to talk of rights invaded ?
And of our beft our deareft blifs difturb'd ?
Thou ! who with more than barbarous perfidy
Haft trampled all allegiance, juftice, truth,
Humanity itfelf, beneath thy feet ?
Thou know'ft thou haft—I could, to thy confufion,
Return thy hard reproaches ; but I fpare thee
Before this lord, for whofe ill-forted friendfhip
Thou haft moft bafely facrific'd thy daughter.
Farewel, my lord !—For thee, lord conftable,
Who doft prefume to lift thy furly eye
To my foft love, my gentle *Sigifmunda*,
I once again command thee, on thy life———
Yes—chew thy rage—but mark me—on thy life,
No further urge thy arrogant pretenfions !

SCENE

SCENE V.

SIFFREDI, OSMOND.

OSMOND.

Ha! arrogant pretenfions! heaven and earth!
What! arrogant pretenfions to my wife?
My wedded wife! Where are we? In a land
Of civil rule, of liberty and laws?——
Not on my life purfue them?—Giddy prince!
My life difdains thy nod. It is the gift
Of parent Heaven, who gave me too an arm,
A fpirit to defend it againft tyrants.
The *Norman* race, the fons of mighty *Rollo*,
Who rufhing in a tempeft from the north,
Great nurfe of generous freemen! bravely won
With their own fwords their feats, and ftill poffefs them
By the fame noble tenure, are not us'd
To hear fuch language—If I now defift,
Then brand me for a coward! deem me villain!
A traitor to the public! By this conduct
Deceiv'd, betray'd, infulted, tyranniz'd.
Mine is a common caufe. My arm fhall guard,
Mix d with my own, the rights of each *Sicilian*,
Of focial life, and of mankind in general.
Ere to thy tyrant rage they fall a prey,
I, fhall find means to fhake thy tottering throne,
Which this illegal, this perfidious ufage

Forfeits at once, and crufh thee in the ruins !—
Conftantia is my queen !

SIFFREDI.

Lord conftable,
Let us be ftedfaft in the right ; but let us
Act with cool prudence, and with manly temper,
As well as manly firmnefs. True, I own,
Th' indignities you fuffer are fo high,
As might even juftify what now you threaten.
But if, my lord, we can prevent the woes,
The cruel horrors of inteftine war,
Yet hold untouch'd our liberties and laws ;
O let us, rais'd above the turbid fphere
Of little felfifh paffions, nobly do it !
Nor to our hot intemperate pride pour out
A dire libation of *Sicilian* blood.
'Tis godlike magnanimity, to keep,
When moft provok'd, our reafon calm and clear,
And execute her will, from a ftrong fenfe
Of what is right, without the vulgar aid
Of heat and paffion, which, tho' honeft, bear us
Often too far.   Remember that my houfe
Protects my daughter ftill ; and ere I faw her
Thus ravifh'd from us, by the arm of power,
This hand fhould act the *Roman* father's part.
Fear not ; be temperate ; all will yet be well.
I know the king.   At firft his paffions burft
Quick as the lightning's flafh ; but in his breaft

Honour

Honour and juſtice dwell—Truſt me, to reaſon
He will return.

OSMOND.

He will!—By Heavens, he ſhall!—
You know the king—I wiſh, my lord *Siffredi*,
That you had deign'd to tell me all you knew—
And would you have me wait, with duteous patience,
Till he return to reaſon ? Ye juſt Powers!
When he has planted on our necks his foot,
And trod us into ſlaves ; when his vain pride
Is cloy'd with our ſubmiſſion ; if, at laſt,
He finds his arm too weak to ſhake the frame
Of wide-eſtabliſh'd order out of joint,
And overturn all juſtice ; then, perchance,
He, in a fit of ſickly kind repentance,
May make a merit to return to reaſon.
No, no, my lord!—There is a nobler way,
To teach the blind oppreſſive *Fury* reaſon :
Oft has the luſtre of avenging ſteel
Unſeal'd her ſtupid eyes—The ſword is reaſon !

I 4   SCENE

SCENE VI.

SIFFREDI, OSMOND, RODOLPHO, *with*
Guards.

RODOLPHO.

My lord high conftable of *Sicily*,
In the king's name, and by his fpecial order,
I here arreft you prifoner of ftate.

OSMOND.

What king ? I know no king of *Sicily*—
Unlefs he be the hufband of *Conftantia*.

RODOLPHO.

Then know him now——Behold his royal orders
To bear you to the caftle of *Palermo*.

SIFFREDI.

Let the big torrent foam its madnefs off.
Submit, my lord—No caftle long can hold
Our wrongs—This, more than friendfhip or alliance,
Confirms me thine ; this binds me to thy fortunes,
By the ftrong tye of common injury,
Which nothing can diffolve——I grieve, *Rodolpho*,
To fee the reign, in fuch unhappy fort,
Begin.

OSMOND.

The reign ! the ufurpation call it !
This meteor king may blaze awhile, but foon
Muft fpend his idle terrors—Sir, lead on——
Farewel,

Farewel, my lord —— More than my life and fortune,
Remember well, is in your hands——my honour!

SIFFREDI.

Our honour is the fame. My fon farewel——
We fhall not long be parted. On thefe eyes
Sleep fhall not fhed his balm, till I behold thee
Reftor'd to freedom, or partake thy bonds.

Even noble courage is not void of blame,
Till nobler patience fanctifies its flame.

The End of the Fourth Act.

A C T

ACT V. SCENE I.

SIFFREDI, *alone.*

THE profpect lowrs around. I found the king,
Tho' calm'd a little, with fubfiding tempeft,
As fuits his generous nature, yet in love
Abated nought, moft ardent in his purpofe ;
Inexorably fix'd, whate'er the rifque,
To claim my daughter, and diffolve this marriage—
I have embark'd, upon a perilous fea,
A mighty treafure. Here the rapid youth,
Th' impetuous paffions of a lover-king
Check my bold courfe; and there, the jealous pride,
Th' impatient honour of a haughty lord
Of the firft rank, in intereft and dependants
Near equal to the king, forbid retreat.
My honour too, the fame unchang'd conviction,
That thefe my meafures were, and ftill remain
Of abfolute neceffity, to fave
The land from civil fury, urge me on.
But how proceed ?—I only fafter rufh
Upon the defperate evils I would fhun.

What

Whate'er the motive be, deceit, I fear,
And harſh unnatural force are not the means
Of public welfare or of private bliſs—
Bear witneſs, Heaven! Thou mind-inſpecting eye!
My breaſt is pure. I have prefer'd my duty,
The good and ſafety of my fellow-ſubjects,
To all thoſe views that fire the ſelfiſh race
Of men, and mix them in eternal broils.

  Enter an OFFICER *belonging to* SIFFREDI.

OFFICER.

My lord, a man of noble port, his face
Wrap'd in diſguiſe, is earneſt for admiſſion.

SIFFREDI.

Go, bid him enter—   [Officer *goes out.*
    Ha! wrap'd in diſguiſe!
And at this late unſeaſonable hour!
When o'er the world tremendous midnight reigns,
By the dire gloom of raging tempeſt doubled—

SCENE II.

SIFFREDI, OSMOND *diſcovering himſelf.*

SIFFREDI.

What! ha! earl *Oſmond*, you?—Welcome, once more,
To this glad roof!— But why in this diſguiſe?
Would I could hope the king exceeds his promiſe!

    I 6.   I have

I have his faith foon as to-morrow's fun
Shall gild *Sicilia*'s cliffs, you fhall be free.——
Has fome good angel turn'd his heart to juftice?

OSMOND.

It is not by the favour of count *Tancred*
That I am here.   As much I fcorn his favour,
As I defy his tyranny and threats———
Our friend *Goffredo*, who commands the caftle,
On my parole, ere dawn, to render back
My perfon, has permitted me this freedom.
Know then ; the faithlefs outrage of to-day,
By him committed whom you call the king,
Has rous'd *Conftantia*'s court. Our friends, the friends
Of virtue, juftice, and of public faith,
Ripe for revolt are in high ferment all.
This. this, they fay, exceeds whate'er deform'd
The miferable days we faw beneath
William the Bad   This faps the folid bafe,
At once, of government and private life ;
This fhamelefs impofition on the faith,
The majefty of fenates this lewd infult,
This violation of the rights of men.
Added to thefe, his ignominious treatment
Of her th' illuftrious offspring of our kings,
Sicilia's hope, and now our royal miftrefs.
You know, my lord, how grofsly thefe infringe
The late king's will ; which orders, if count *Tancred*
Make not *Conftantia* partner of his throne,
That he be quite excluded the fucceffion,

                                             And

And she to *Henry* given, king of the *Romans*,
The potent emperor *Barbaroſſa*'s ſon,
Who ſeeks with earneſt inſtance her alliance.
I thence of you, as guardian of the laws,
As guardian of this Will to you entruſted,
Deſire, nay more, demand your inſtant aid,
To ſee it put in vigorous execution.

SIFFREDI.

You cannot doubt, my lord, of my concurrence.
Who more than I have labour'd this great point ?
'Tis my own plan. And, if I drop it now,
I ſhould be juſtly branded with the ſhame
Of raſh advice, or deſpicable weakneſs.
But let us not precipitate the matter.
Conſtantia's friends are numerous and ſtrong ;
Yet *Tancred*'s, truſt me, are of equal force.
E'er ſince the ſecret of his birth was known,
The people all are in a tumult hurl'd
Of boundleſs joy, to hear there lives a prince
Of mighty *Guiſcard*'s line. Numbers. beſides,.
Of powerful barons, who at heart had pin'd,
To ſee the reign of their renown'd forefathers,.
Won by immortal deeds of matchleſs valour,.
Paſs from the gallant *Normans* to the *Suevi*,
Will with a kind of rage eſpouſe his cauſe—
'Tis ſo, my lord—be not by paſſion blinded——
'Tis ſurely ſo—O if our prating virtue
Dwells not in words alone—O let us join,
My generous *Oſmond*, to avert theſe woes,

I

And yet fuftain our tottering *Norman* kingdom !.

OSMOND.

But how, *Siffredi ?* how ?—If by foft means
We can maintain our rights, and fave our country,.
May his unnatural blood firft ftain the fword,
Who with unpitying fury firft fhall draw it !

SIFFREDI.

I have a thought—The glorious work be thine:.
But it requires an awful flight of virtue,
Above the paffions of the vulgar breaft,.
And thence from thee I hope it, noble *Ofmond*—.
Suppofe my daughter, to her God devoted,
Were plac'd within fome convent's facred verge;
Beneath the dread protection of the altar—

OSMOND.

Ere then, by Heavens ! I would devoutly fhave
My holy fcalp, turn whining monk myfelf,
And pray inceffant for the tyrant's fafety !—
What ! How ! becaufe an infolent invader,
A facrilegious tyrant, in contempt
Of all thofe nobleft rights, which to maintain
Is man's peculiar pride, demands my wife ;
That I fhall thus betray the common caufe
Of human kind, and tamely yield her up,
Even in the manner you propofe—O then
I were fupremely vile ! degraded ! fham'd !·
The fcorn of manhood ! and abhor'd of honour !

SIFFREDI.

There is, my lord, an honour, the calm child

Of

Of reafon, of humanity and mercy,
Superior far to this punctilious demon,
That fingly minds itfelf, and oft embroils
With proud barbarian niceties the world !

OSMOND.

My lord, my lord!—I cannot brook your prudence—
It holds a pulfe unequal to my blood——
Unblemifh'd honour is the flower of virtue !
The vivifying foul ! and he who flights it
Will leave the other dull and lifelefs drofs.

SIFFREDI.

No more——You are too warm.

OSMOND.

You are too cool.

SIFFREDI.

Too cool, my lord ? I were indeed too cool,
Not to refent this language, and to tell thee——
I wifh earl *Ofmond* were as cool as I
To his own felfifh blifs—ay, and as warm
To that of others—But of this no more——
My daughter is thy wife—I gave her to thee,
And will againft all force maintain her thine.
But think not I will catch thy headlong paffions,
Whirl'd in a blaze of madnefs o'er the land ;
Or, till the laft extremit, compel me,
Rifque the dire means of war—The king to-morrow,
Will fet you free ; and, if by gentle means
He does not yield my daughter to your arms,
And wed *Conftantia*, as the will requires,

Why

Why then expect me on the side of justice——
Let that suffice.

OSMOND.

It does—Forgive my heat,·
My rankled mind, by injuries inflam'd,
May be too prompt to take and give offence.·

SIFFREDI.

'Tis past—Your wrongs, I own, may well transport'
The wisest mind—But henceforth, noble *Osmond*,
Do me more justice, honour more my truth,
Nor mark me with an eye of squint suspicion——
These jars apart—You may repose your soul
On my firm faith and unremitting friendship.
Of that I sure have given exalted proof,
And the next sun we see, shall prove it further——
Return, my son, and from your friend *Goffredo·*
Release your word. There try, by soft repose,·
To calm your breast.

OSMOND.

Bid the vext ocean sleep,·
Swept by the pinions of the raging north——
But your frail age, by care and toil exhausted,·
Demands the balm of all-repairing rest.

SIFFREDI.

Soon as to-morrow's dawn shall streak the skies,·
I, with my friends in solemn state assembled,
Will to the palace, and demand your freedom,·
Then by calm reason, or by higher means,
The king shall quit his claim, and in the face

Of·

Of *Sicily*, my daughter fhall be yours.
Farewel.

OSMOND.

My lord, good night.

SCENE III.

OSMOND *alone.* [*After a long paufe.*
I like him not————

Yes—I have mighty matter of fufpicion.
'Tis plain—I fee it lurking in his breaft,
He has a foolifh fondnefs for this king—
My honour is not fafe, while here my wife
Remains—Who knows but he this very night
May bear her to fome convent as he mention'd—
The king too—tho' I fmother'd up my rage,
I mark'd it well—will fet me free to-morrow.
Why not to-night? He has fome dark defign—
By Heavens! he has—I am abus'd moft grofsly;
Made the vile tool of this old ftatefman's fchemes;
Marry'd to one—Ay, and he knew it,—one
Who loves young *Tancred!* Hence her fwooning, tears,
And all her foft diftrefs, when fhe difgrac'd me
By bafely giving her perfidious hand
Without her heart—Hell and perdition! this,
This is the perfidy!—This is the fell,
The keen, envenom'd, exquifite difgrace!

Which

Which to a man of honour even exceeds
The falfehood of the perfon—But I now
Will roufe me from the poor tame lethargy,
By my believing fondnefs caft upon me.
I will not wait his crawling timid motions,
Perhaps to blind me meant, which he to-morrow
Has promis'd to purfue. No! ere his eyes
Shall open on to-morrow's orient beam,
I will convince him that earl *Ofmond* never
Was form'd to be his dupe—I know full well
Th' important weight and danger of the deed:
But to a man, whom greater dangers prefs,
Driven to the brink of infamy and horror,
Rafhnefs itfelf, and utter defperation,
Are the beft prudence—I will bear her off
This night, and lodge her in a place of fafety.
I have a trufty band that waits not far.
Hence! let me lofe no time—One rapid moment
Should ardent form, at once, and execute
A bold defign—'Tis fix'd—'Tis done!—Yes, then,
When I have feiz'd the prize of love and honour,
And with a friend fecur'd her; to the caftle
I will repair, and claim *Geffredo*'s promife
To rife with all his garrifon—my friends
With brave impatience wait. The mine is laid,
And only wants my kindling touch to fpring.

SCENE

SCENE IV.

SIGISMUNDA's *Apartment.*

SIGISMUNDA, LAURA.

LAURA.

Heavens! 'tis a fearful night!

SIGISMUNDA.

                  Ah! the black rage
Of midnight tempeſt, or th' aſſuring ſmiles
Of radiant morn are equal all to me.
Nought now has charms or terrors to my breaſt,
The ſeat of ſtupid woe!—Leave me, my *Laura.*
Kind reſt, perhaps, may huſh my woes a little—
Oh for that quiet ſleep that knows no morning!

LAURA.

Madam, indeed I know not how to go.
Indulge my fondneſs—Let me watch a while
By your ſad bed, till theſe dread hours ſhall paſs.

SIGISMUNDA.

Alas! what is the toil of elements,   .
This idle perturbation of the ſky,
To what I feel within!—Oh that the fires
Of pitying Heaven would point their fury here!
Good night, my deareſt *Laura!*

LAURA.

             O I know not

                What

What this oppreſſion means—But 'tis with pain,
With tears, I can perſuade myſelf to leave you—
Well then—Good night, my deareſt *Sigiſmunda !*

***

SCENE V.

SIGISMUNDA.

And am I then alone ?—The moſt undone,
Moſt wretched being now beneath the cope
Of this affrighting gloom that wraps the world!——
I ſaid I did not fear—Ah me! I feel
A ſhivering horror run thro' all my powers !
O I am nought but tumult, fears and weakneſs!
And yet how idle fear when hope is gone,
Gone, gone for ever !—O thou gentle ſcene
     [*Looking towards her bed.*
Of ſweet repoſe, where by th' oblivious draught
Of each ſad toilſome day, to peace reſtor'd
Unhappy mortals loſe their woes awhile,
Thou haſt no peace for me '—What ſhall I do ?
How paſs this dreadful night, ſo big with terror ?—
Here, with the midnight ſhades, here will I ſit,
     [*Sitting down.*
A prey to dire deſpair, and ceaſeleſs weep
The hours away—Bleſs me—I heard a noiſe——
     [*Starting up.*
No—I miſtook—Nothing but ſilence reigns
       And

And awful midnight round—Again !—O Heavens!
My lord the king !

SCENE VI.

TANCRED, SIGISMUNDA.

TANCRED.

Be not alarm'd, my love!

SIGISMUNDA.

My royal lord ! why at this midnight hour,
How came you hither ?

TANCRED.

By that fecret way
My love contriv'd, when we, in happier days,
Us'd to devote thefe hours, fo much in vain,
To vows of love and everlafting friendfhip.

SIGISMUNDA.

Why will you thus perfift to add new ftings
To her diftrefs, who never can be thine ?
O fly me ! fly ! You know——

TANCRED.

I know too much.
O how I could reproach thee, *Sigifmunda !*
Pour out my injur'd foul in juft complaints !
But now the time permits not, thefe fwift moments—
I told thee how thy father's artifice
Forc'd me to feem perfidious in thy eyes.

Ah,

Ah, fatal blindnefs! not to have obferv'd
The mingled pangs of rage and love that fhook me :
When, by my cruel public fituation
Compell'd, I only feign'd confent, to gain
A little time, and more fecure thee mine.
E'er fince—A dreadful interval of care !
My thoughts have been employ'd, not without hope,
How to defeat *Siffredi*'s barbarous purpofe.
But thy credulity has ruin'd all,
Thy rafh, thy wild—I know not what to name it——
Oh, it has prov'd the giddy hopes of man
To be delufion all, and fickening folly !

SIGISMUNDA.

Ah, generous *Tancred !* ah thy truth deftroys me !
Yes, yes, 'tis I, 'tis I alone am falfe !
My hafty rage, join'd to my tame fubmiffion,
More than the moft exalted filial duty
Could e'er demand, has dafh'd our cup of fate
With bitternefs unequal'd—But, alas !
What are thy woes to mine?—to mine! juft Heaven!—
Now is thy turn of vengeance—hate, renounce me !
O leave me to the fate I well deferve,
To fink in hopelefs mifery !—at leaft,
Try to forget the worthlefs *Sigifmunda !*

TANCRED.

Forget thee ! No ! Thou art my foul itfelf !
I have no thought, no hope, no wifh but thee !
Even this repented injury, the fears,
That roufe me all to madnefs, at the thought

Of

Of lofing thee, the whole collected pains
Of my full heart, ferve but to make thee dearer!
Ah, how forget thee!—Much muft be forgot,
Ere *Tancred* can forget his *Sigifmunda!*

SIGISMUNDA.

But you, my lord, muft make that great effort.

TANCRED.

Can *Sigifmunda* make it?

SIGISMUNDA.

    Ah! I know not
With what fuccefs—But all that feeble woman
And love-entangled reafon can perform,
I, to the utmoft, will exert to do it.

TANCRED.

Fear not—'Tis done!—If thou canft form the thought,
Succefs is fure—I am forgot already!

SIGISMUNDA.

Ah *Tancred!*—But, my lord, refpect me more.
Think who I am—What can you now propofe?

TANCRED.

To claim the plighted vows which Heaven has heard,
To vindicate the rights of holy love
By faith and honour bound, to which compar'd
Thefe empty forms, which have enfnar'd thy hand,
Are impious guile abufe, and profanation——
Nay, as a king. whofe high prerogative
By this unlicens'd marriage is affronted,
To bid the laws themfelves pronounce it void.

SIGIS-

SIGISMUNDA.

Honour, my lord, is much too proud to catch
At every flender twig of nice diftinctions.
Thefe for th' unfeeling vulgar may do well:
But thofe, whofe fouls are by the nicer rule
Of virtuous delicacy nobly fway'd,
Stand at another bar than that of laws.
Then ceafe to urge me—Since I am not born
To that exalted fate to be your queen—
Or, yet a dearer name—to be your wife!———
I am the wife of an illuftrious lord
Of your own princely blood; and what I am,
I will with proper dignity remain.
Retire, my royal lord—There is no means
To cure the wounds this fatal day has given.
We meet no more!

TANCRED.

Oh barbarous *Sigifmunda!*
And canft thou talk thus fteadily? thus treat me
With fuch unpitying, unrelenting rigour?
Poor is the love, that rather than give up
A little pride, a little formal pride,
The breath of vanity! can bear to fee
The man, whofe heart was once fo dear to thine
By many a tender vow fo mix'd together,
A prey to anguifh, fury and diftraction!—
Thou canft not furely make me fuch a wretch,
Thou canft not, *Sigifmunda!*—Yet relent,
O fave us yet!—*Redolpho*, with my guards,

Waits,

Waits in the garden—Let us feize the moments
We ne'er may have again—With more than power
I will affert thee mine, with faireft honour.
The world fhall even approve ; each honeft bofom
Swell with a kindred joy to fee us happy.

SIGISMUNDA.

The world approve ! What is the world to me ?
The confcious mind is its own awful world.——
And yet, perhaps, if thou wert not a king,
I know not, *Tancred*, what I might have done,
Then, then, my conduct, fanctify'd by love,
Could not be deem'd, by the fevereft judge,
The mean effect of intereft or ambition.
But now not all my partial heart can plead,
Shall ever fhake th' unalterable dictates
That tyrannize my breaft.

TANCRED.

'Tis well—No more—
I yield me to my fate—Yes, yes inhuman !
Since thy barbarian heart is fteel'd by pride,
Shut up to love and pity, here behold me
Caft on the ground, a vile and abject wretch !
Loft to all cares, all dignities, all duties !
Here will I grow, breathe out my faithful foul,
Here at thy feet—Death, death alone fhall part us !

SIGISMUNDA.

Have you then vow'd to drive me to perdition ?
What can I more ?—Yes, *Tancred !* once again
I will forget the dignity my ftation

VOL. IV.　　　K　　　　　Com-

Commands me to fuſtain—for the laſt time
Will tell thee, that, I fear, no ties, no duty,
Can ever root thee from my haplefs boſom.
O leave me! fly me! were it but in pity!—
To ſee what once we tenderly have lov'd,
Cut off from every hope—cut off for ever!
Is pain thy generoſity ſhould ſpare me.
Then riſe, my lord; and if you truly love me;
If you reſpect my honour, nay, my peace,
Retire! for tho' th' emotions of my heart
Can ne'er alarm my virtue; yet, alas!
They tear it ſo, they pierce it with ſuch anguiſh—
Oh, 'tis too much!—I cannot bear the conflict!

S C E N E VII.

TANCRED, OSMOND, SIGISMUNDA.

OSMOND, *entering*.

Turn, tyrant! turn! and anſwer to my honour,
For this thy baſe inſufferable outrage!

TANCRED.

Inſolent traitor! think not to eſcape
Thyſelf my vengeance! [*They fight. Oſmond falls.*

SIGISMUNDA.

Help here! Help!—O Heavens!
[*Throwing herſelf down by him.*

Alas! my lord, what meant your headlong rage?

That

That faith, which I this day, upon the altar,
To you devoted, is unblemiſh'd, pure,
As veſtal truth ; was reſolutely yours,
Beyond the power of aught on earth to ſhake it.

OSMOND.

Perfidious woman ! die !————

[*Shortning his ſword, he plunges it into her breaſt.*
and to the grave
Attend a huſband, yet but half aveng'd !

TANCRED.

O horror ! horror ! execrable villain !

OSMOND.

And, tyrant ! thou !—Thou ſhalt not o'er my tomb
Exult—'Tis well—'Tis great !—I die content !—

[*Dies.*

SCENE VIII.

TANCRED, SIFFREDI, RODOLPHO, SIGIS-MUNDA, LAURA.

TANCRED.

[*Throwing himſelf down by* Sigiſmunda.
Quick ! here ! bring aid !—All in *Palermo* bring
Whoſe ſkill can ſave her !—Ah ! that gentle boſom
Pours faſt the ſtreams of life.

SIGISMUNDA.

All aid is vain,
I feel the powerful hand of death upon me—

K 2

But,

But, oh! it fheds a fweetnefs thro' my fate,
That I am thine again ; and without blame,
May in my *Tancred's* arms refign my foul!

TANCRED.

Oh, death is in that voice! fo gently mild,
So fadly fweet, as mixes even with mine
The tears of hovering angels!—Mine again!——
And is it thus the cruel Fates have join'd us?
Are thefe the horrid nuptials they prepare
For love like ours? Is virtue thus rewarded?
Let not my impious rage accufe juft Heaven!
Thou, *Tancred!* Thou! haft murder'd *Sigifmunda!*
That furious man was but the tool of Fate,
I, I the caufe!—But I will do thee juftice
On this deaf heart! that to thy tender wifdom
Refus'd an ear—Yes, death fhall foon unite us!

SIGISMUNDA.

Live, live, my *Tancred!*—Let my death fuffice
To expiate all that may have been amifs.
May it appeafe the Fates, avert their fury
From thy propitious reign! Mean-time, of me
And of thy glory mindful, live, I charge thee,
To guard our friends, and make thy people happy—

[*Obferving* Siffredi *fixt in aftonifhment and grief.*

My father!——Oh! how fhall I lift my eyes
To thee my finking father!

SIFFREDI.

Awful Heaven!
I am chaftis'd —— My deareft child!——

6   SIGIS-

SIGISMUNDA.

Where am I?
A fearful darknefs clofes all around—
My friends! We needs muft part—I muft obey
Th' imperious call!—Farewel, my *Laura*! cherifh
My poor afflicted father's age—*Rodolpho*,
Now is the time to watch th' unhappy king,
With all the care and tendernefs of friendfhip—
Oh my dear father! bow'd beneath the weight
Of age and grief—the victim even of virtue,
Receive my laft adieu!—Where art thou, *Tancred?*
Give me thy hand—But, ah!—it cannot fave me
From the dire king of terrors, whofe cold power
Creeps o'er my heart——Oh!

TANCRED.

How thefe pangs diftract me!
O lift thy gracious eyes;——Thou leav'ft me then!
Thou leav'ft me, *Sigifmunda!*

SIGISMUNDA.

Yet a moment—
I had, my *Tancred*, fomething more to fay——
Yes——but thy love and tendernefs for me
Sure makes it needlefs—Harbour no refentment
Againft my father; venerate his zeal,
That acted from a principle of goodnefs,
From faithful love to thee—Live, and maintain
My innocence imbalm'd, with holieft care
Preferve my fpotlefs memory!——I die——
ETERNAL MERCY take my trembling foul!

K 3   Oh!

Oh! 'tis the only fting of death to part
From thofe we love—from thee—farewel, my *Tancred!*   [*Dies.*

TANCRED.

Thus then!

[*Flying to his favord, is held by* Rodolpho.

RODOLPHO.

Hold! hold! my lord!—Have you forgot
Your *Sigifmunda's* laft requeft already?

TANCRED.

Off! fet me free! Think not to bind me down,
With barbarous friendfhip, to the rack of life!
What hand can fhut the thoufand thoufand gates,
Which death ftill opens to the woes of mortals?—
I fhall find means—No power in earth or heaven
Can force me to endure the hateful light,
Thus robb'd of all that lent it joy and fweetnefs!
Off! traitors! off! or my diftracted foul
Will burft indignant from this jail of nature,
To where fhe beckons yonder—No, mild feraph!
Point not to life——I cannot linger here,
Cut off from thee, the miferable pity,
The fcorn of human kind!——A trampled king!
Who let his mean poor-hearted love, one moment,
To coward prudence ftoop; who made it not
The firft undoubting action of his reign,
To fnatch thee to his throne, and there to fhield thee,
Thy helplefs bofom from a ruffian's fury!——
O fhame! O agony! O the fell ftings

Of

Of late, of vain repentance!——Ha! my brain
Is all on fire! a wild abyſs of thought!
Th' infernal world diſcloſes! See! behold him!
Lo! with fierce ſiniles he ſhakes the bloody ſteel,
And mocks my feeble tears!—Hence! quickly,
       hence!
Spurn his vile carcaſs! give it to the dogs!
Expoſe it to the winds and ſcreaming ravens!
Or hurl it down that fiery ſteep to hell,
There with his ſoul to toſs in flames for ever!——
Ah, impotence of rage!—What am I? Where?
Sad, ſilent, all?—The forms of dumb deſpair,
Around ſome mournful tomb!—What do I ſee?
This ſoft abode of innocence and love
Turn'd to the houſe of death! a place of horror!——
Ah! that poor corſe! pale! pale! deform'd with murder!
Is that my *Sigiſmunda!*

                [*Throwing himſelf down by her.*

        SIFFREDI.

[*After a pathetic pauſe, looking on the ſcene before him.*
        Have I liv'd

To theſe enfeebled years, by Heaven reſerv'd,
To be a dreadful monument of juſtice?——
Rodolpho, raiſe the king, and bear him hence
From this diſtracting ſcene of blood and death.
Alas! I dare not give him my aſſiſtance;
My care would only more enflame his rage.

  Behold the fatal work of my dark hand,
That by rude force the paſſions would command,

        K 4   That

That ruthless fought to root them from the breast;
They may be rul'd, but will not be opprest.
Taught hence, ye parents, who from nature stray,
And the great ties of social life betray;
Ne'er with your children act a tyrant's part:
'Tis yours to guide, not violate the heart:
Ye vainly wife, who o'er mankind preside,
Behold my righteous woes, and drop your pride!
Keep Virtue's fimple path before your eyes,
Nor think from evil good can ever rife.

The End of the Fifth Act.

EPILOGUE.

EPILOGUE.

Spoken by Mifs BUDGELL.

CRamm'd to the throat with wholefome moral ftuff,
Alas! poor audience! you have had enough.
Was ever haplefs heroine of a play
In fuch a piteous plight as ours to-day?
Was ever woman fo by love betray'd?
Match'd with two hufbands, and yet—die a maid.
But blefs me!—hold—What founds are thefe I hear!—
I fee the Tragic Mufe herfelf appear.

The back-fcene opens, and difcovers a romantic
Sylvan landfkip; from which Mrs. *Cibber*, in the
character of the Tragic Mufe, advances flowly to
mufic, and fpeaks the following lines:

Hence with your flippant epilogue, that tries
To wipe the virtuous tear from Britifh eyes;
That dares my moral, tragic fcene profane,
With ftrains—at beft, unfuiting, light and vain.

Hence

Hence from the pure unfully'd beams that play
In yon fair eyes where virtue shines--Away!
 Britons, to you from chaste Castalian groves,
Where dwell the tender, oft unhappy loves;
Where shades of heroes roam, each mighty name,
And court my aid to rise again to fame;
To you I come, to freedom's noblest seat,
And in Britannia fix my last retreat.
 In Greece and Rome, I watch'd the public weal;
The purple tyrant trembled at my steel:
Nor did I less o'er private sorrows reign,
And mend the melting heart with softer pain.
On France and You then rose my brightning star,
With social ray—The Arts are ne'er at war.
O, as your fire and genius stronger blaze,
As yours are generous Freedom's bolder lays,
Let not the Gallic taste leave yours behind,
In decent manners and in life refin'd;
Banish the motly mode, to tag low verse,
The laughing ballad to the mournful herse.
When thro' five acts your hearts have learnt to glow,
Touch'd with the sacred force of honest woe;
O keep the dear impression on your breast,
Nor idly lose it for a wretched jest.

CORIO-

Coriolanus.

G. V. Neal sc.

CORIOLANUS.

A

TRAGEDY.

PROLOGUE.

Written by

The Hon. GEORGE LYTTELTON, Efq;

Spoken by Mr. QUIN.

I *Come not here your candour to implore*
    For ſcenes, whoſe author is, alas! no more ;
He wants no advocate his cauſe to plead ;
You will yourſelves be patrons of the dead.
No party his benevolence confin'd,
No ſect—alike it flow'd to all mankind.
He lov'd his friends (forgive this guſhing tear :
Alas! I feel I am no actor here)
He lov'd his friends with ſuch a warmth of heart,
So clear of int'reſt, ſo devoid of art,
Such generous friendſhip, ſuch unſhaken zeal,
No words can ſpeak it, but our tears may tell.——
O candid truth, O faith without a ſtain,
O manners gently firm, and nobly plain,
O ſympathizing love of others bliſs,
Where will you find another breaſt like his?
Such was the man—the poet well you know :
Oft has he touch'd your hearts with tender woe :

Oft

Oft in this crowded house, with just applause,
You heard him teach fair Virtue's purest laws;
For his chaste muse employ'd her heav'n-taught lyre
None but the noblest passions to inspire,
Not one immoral, one corrupted thought,
One line, which dying he could wish to blot.
O!, may to-night your favourable doom
Another laurel add to grace his tomb:
Whilst he, superior now to praise or blame,
Hears not the feeble voice of human fame.
Yet if to those, whom most on earth he lov'd,
From whom his pious care is now remov'd,
With whom his liberal hand, and bounteous heart,
Shar'd all his little fortune could impart;
If to those friends your kind regard shall give
What they no longer can from his receive,
That, that, even now, above yon starry pole,
May touch with pleasure his immortal soul.

The

The Persons represented.

CAIUS MARCIUS CORIOLANUS,   Mr. *Quin*.

ATTIUS TULLUS, general of the } Mr. *Ryan*.
Volscian army,

GALESUS, one of the deputies of }
the *Volscian* states attending the } Mr. *Delane*.
camp,

The other Deputies of the *Volscian*
states.

VOLUSIUS, one of the principal } Mr. *Sparks*.
Volscian officers,

TITUS, freed-man of *Galesus*,   Mr. *Ridout*.

MARCUS MINUCIUS, consul and }
principal of the deputation from } Mr. *Bridgwater*.
Rome to *Corio'anus*,

POSTHUMUS COMINIUS, a consular }
senator, one of the deputation, } Mr. *Anderson*.
and who had been the *Roman* }
general at the taking of *Corioli*, }

VETURIA, mother of *Coriolanus*,   Mrs. *Woffington*,
VOLUMNIA, wife of *Coriolanus*,   Miss *Bellamy*.

Roman Senators, Priests, Augurs, &c. of the first deputation. *Roman* Ladies in the train of *Veturia*
and *Volumnia*, of the second deputation.

Volscian OFFICERS, LICTORS, SOLDIERS, &c.

SCENE, *The* Volscian *Camp*.

CORIOLANUS.

A

TRAGEDY.

ACT I. SCENE I.

The Volscian *Camp.*

ATTIUS TULLUS, VOLUSIUS.

VOLUSIUS.

WHence is it, *Tullus*, that our arms are ſtopt
Here on the borders of the *Roman* ſtate?
Why ſleeps that ſpirit, whoſe heroic ardor
Urg'd you to break the truce, and pour'd our hoſt,
From all th' united cantons of the *Volſci*,

On

On their unguarded frontier ? Such defigns
Brook not an hour's delay ; their whole fuccefs
Depends on inftant vigorous execution.

TULLUS.

Velufius, I approve thy brave impatience ;
And will to thee, in confidence of friendfhip,
Difclofe my fecret foul. Thou know'ft *Galefus*,
Whofe freedom *Caius Marcius*, once his guelt,
Of all the fpoil of fack'd *Corioli*,
Alone demanded ; and who thence to *Rome*,
From gratitude and friendfhip, followed *Marcius*;
Whence lately to our *Antium* he return'd,
With overtures of peace propos'd by *Rome*,.

VOLUSIUS.

I know him well; an antiquated fage
Of that romantic fchool *Pythagoras*
Eftablifh'd here on our *Hefperian* fhore;
Whofe gentle dictates only ferve to tame
Enfeebled mortals into flaves.

TULLUS.

Galefus,

Doubtlefs, poffeffes many civil virtues;
Is gentle, good ; for rectitude of heart,
And innocence of life by all rever'd.

VOLUSIUS.

Pardon me, *Tullus*, if my faithful bluntnefs
Deems you too liberal in his praife. In peace
Such may perhaps do well, when prating rules
An idle world ; but in tempeftuous times

They

They are ſtark naught, theſe viſionary ſtateſmen,
Fit rulers only for their golden age.
The rugged genius of rapacious *Rome*
For other men, and other counſels, calls.

TULLUS.

Your thoughts are mine—I only meant to tell thee
The part he bears in this ill-tim'd delay.

Soon as our gather'd army march'd from *Antium,*
The *Roman* ſenate, whoſe attentive caution
Watch'd all our motions, took at once th' alarm;
And ſent a herald, ere we paſs'd their borders,
With formal ceremony, to demand
The cauſe of our approach.—Had I been maſter,
I would have anſwer'd at the gates of *Rome.*
But this *Galeſus,* who attends our camp
Among the *Volſcian* deputies, ſo pleaded
The laws of nations, made ſuch loud complaints
Againſt th' infraction of the public faith,
So teaz'd us with the pedantry of ſtates,
That I was forc'd, unwilling, to permit
His freedman *Titus,* to be ſent to *Rome*
With our demands. If theſe the ſenate grants,
We then are in the toils of peace entangled,
In ſpite of all my efforts to avoid them.

VOLUSIUS.

O, 'tis a wild chimera! Peace with *Rome!*
Dream not of that, unleſs the *Volſcian* courage
Is quite ſubdu'd, and only ſeeks to gild
A vile ſubmiſſion with that ſpecious name.

Learn

Learn wifdom from your neighbours. Peace with *Rome*
Has quell'd the *Latines*, tam'd their free-born fpirit,
And by her friendfhip honour'd them with chains.

TULLUS.

She ne'er will grant it on the juft conditions
I now have brought the *Volfci* to demand:
The reftitution of our conquer'd cities,
And fair alliance upon equal terms.
I know the *Roman* infolence will fcorn
To yield to this: and *Titus* muft return,
Within three days, the longeft term allow'd him;
Of which the third is near elaps'd already.
Then even *Galefus* will not dare to ftop us
With fuperftitious forms, and folemn trifles,
From letting loofe th' unbridled rage of war
Againft thofe hated tyrants of *Hefperia*.

VOLUSIUS.

Thanks to the gods! my fword will then be free;
Then, poor *Corioli!* thy bleeding wounds,
Thy treafures fack'd, thy captive matrons,
Shall amply be reveng'd by thy *Volufius*:
Then, *Tullus*, from the lofty brows of *Marcius*
Thou may'ft regain the wreaths his conquering hand,
By partial fortune aided, tore from thine.

TULLUS.

O my *Volufius!* thou, who art a foldier,
A try'd and brave one too, fay, in thy heart
Doft thou not fcorn me? thou, who faw'ft me bend
Beneath the half-fpent thunder of a foe,

Warm

Warm from the conqueſt of *Corioli*,
Which, ruſhing furious in with thoſe, whoſe ſally
He had repell'd, he ſeiz'd almoſt alone ;
And gave to fire and ſword. Yet thence he flew,
Scorning the plunder of our richeſt city,
His wounds undreſt, without a moment's reſpite,
To where our armies on the fearful edge
Of battle ſtood ; and, aſking of the conſul
To be oppos'd to me, with mighty rage,
Reſiſtleſs, bore us down.

VOLUSIUS.

        True valour, *Tullus*,
Lies in the mind, the never-yielding purpoſe,
Nor owns the blind award of giddy Fortune.

TULLUS.

My ſoul, my friend, my ſoul is all on fire !
Thirſt of revenge conſumes me ! the revenge
Of generous emulation, not of hatred
This happy *Roman*, this proud *Marcius* haunts me.
Each troubled night when ſlaves and captives ſleep,
Forgetful of their chains, I, in my dreams,
Anew am vanquiſh'd ; and, beneath the ſword
With horror ſinking, feel a tenfold death,
The death of honour. But I will redeem—
Yes, *Marcius*, I will yet redeem my fame.
To face thee once again is the great purpoſe
For which alone I live —Till then how ſlow,
How tedious lags the time ! while ſhame corrodes me,
With many a bitter thought ; and injur'd honour
Sick, and deſponding, preys upon itſelf.

VOLUSIUS.

VOLUSIUS.

It fast approaches now, the hour of vengeance,
To this fam'd land, to ancient *Latium* due.
Unbalanc'd *Rome*, at variance with herself,
To order lost, in deep and hot commotion,
Stands on the dangerous point of civil war ;
Her haughty nobles, and seditious commons
Reviling, fearing, hating one another :
While, on our part, all wears a prosperous face ;
Our troops united, numerous, high in spirit,
As if their gen'ral's soul inform'd them all.
O long-expected day !

TULLUS.

Go, brave *Volusius,*
Go breathe thy ardor into every breast,
That when the *Velscian* envoy shall return,
Whom ere the close of evening I expect,
One spirit may unite us in the cause
Of generous freedom, and our native rights,
So long oppress'd by *Rome*'s encroaching power.

SCENE II.

TULLUS *alone.*

Galesus said that *Marcius* stands for consul.
O favour thou his suit, propitious *Jove !*
That I may brave him at his army's head,
In all the majesty of sovereign pow'r !

5   That

That the whole conduct of the war may rest
On us alone, and prove by its decision,
Which of the two is worthiest to command——

SCENE III.

TULLUS, OFFICER.

TULLUS.

Ha! why this haste? you look alarm'd.

OFFICER.

My lord,

One of exalted port, his visage hid,
Has plac'd himself upon your sacred hearth,
Beneath the dread protection of your *Lares*;
And sits majestic there in solemn silence.

TULLUS.

Did you not ask him who, and what he was?

OFFICER.

My lord, I could not speak; I felt appall'd,
As if the presence of some God had struck me.

TULLUS.

Come, dastard! let me find this man of terrors.

SCENE

SCENE IV.

The back-scene opens, and discovers CORIOLANUS *as described above.*

CORIOLANUS, TULLUS.

TULLUS, *after some silence.*
Illustrious stranger—for thy high demeanour
Bespeaks thee such—who art thou?

CORIOLANUS.
[*Rising and unmuffling his face.*
View me, *Tullus*—
[*After some pause.*

Dost thou not know me?

TULLUS.
No.   That noble front
I never saw before.   What is thy name?

CORIOLANUS.
Does not the secret voice of hostile instinct,
Does not thy swelling heart declare me to thee?

TULLUS.
Gods! can it be?—

CORIOLANUS.
Yes.   I am *Caius Marcius*;
Known to thy smarting country by the name
Of *Coriolanus*.   That alone is left me,
That empty name, for all my toils, my service,

The

The blood which I have fhed for thanklefs *Rome*.
Behold me banifh'd thence, a victim yielded
By her weak nobles to the maddening rabble.
I feek revenge. Thou may'ft employ my fword,
With keener edge, with heavier force againft her,
Than e'er it fell upon the *Volfcian* nation.
But if thou, *Tullus*, doft refufe me this,
The only wifh of my collected heart,
Where every paffion in one burning point
Concenters, give me death : Death from thy hand
I fure have well deferv'd—Nor fhall I blufh
To take or life or death from *Attius Tullus*.

TULLUS.

O *Caius Marcius !* in this one fhort moment,
That we have friendly talk'd, my ravifh'd heart
Has undergone a great, a wonderous change.
I ever held thee in my beft efteem ;
But this heroic confidence has won me,
Stampt me at once thy friend. I were indeed
A wretch as mean as this thy truft is noble,
Could I refufe thee thy demand—Yes, *Marcius !*
Thou haft thy wifh ! take half of my command,
If that be not enough, then take the whole.
We have, my friend, a gallant force on foot,
An army, *Marcius*, fit to follow thee.
Go lead them on, and take thy full revenge.
All fhould unite to punifh the ungrateful,
Ingratitude is treafon to mankind.

CORIOLANUS, *embracing him.*

Thus, generous *Tullus*, take a soldier's thanks,
Who is not practis'd in the glofs of words——
Thou friend in deed! friend to my caufe, my quarrel!
Friend to the darling paffion of my foul!
All elfe I fet at nought!—Immortal gods!
I am new-made, and wonder at myfelf!
A little while ago, and I was nothing;
A powerlefs reptile, crawling on the earth,
Curs'd with a foul that reftlefs wifh'd to wield
The bolts of *Jove!* I dwelt in *Erebus*,
I wander'd thro' the hopelefs gloom of hell,
Stung with revenge, tormented by the furies!
Now, *Tullus*, like a god, you draw me thence,
'Throne me amidft the fkies, with tempeft charg'd,
And put the ready thunder in my hand!

TULLUS.

What I have promis'd, *Marcius*, I will do.
Within an hour at fartheft we expect
The freedman of *Cakfus* back from *Rome*,
Who carried to the fenate our demands.
Their anfwer will, I doubt not, end the truce,
And inftant draw our angry fwords againft them.
Till then retire within my inmoft tent,
Unknown to all but me, that when our chiefs
Meet in full council to declare for war,
I may produce thee to their wondering eyes,
As if defcended from avenging Heaven

7   To

To humble lofty *Rome*, and teach her juftice.

CORIOLANUS.

To thy direction, *Tullus*, I refign
My future life : my fate is in thy hands ;
And, if I judge aright, the fate of *Rome*.

.

-

The End of the Firſt Act.

ACT II. SCENE I.

GALESUS, TITUS.

GALESUS.

INDEED! my *Titus*, I had hopes that *Rome*,
Vext as she is with her domestic broils,
Her frontier weak, her armies unprepar'd,
Might have comply'd with our demands, and given us
The same alliance granted to the *Latines*.

TITUS.

The senate scarce would hear the terms I offer'd;
But order'd me to bear this answer back:
" If first the *Volsci* take up arms, the *Romans*
" Will be the last to lay them down."

GALESUS.

Alas!
This answer seals the doom of many a wretch.
Unchain'd *Bellona* from her temple rushes,
With all the crimes and vices in her train.
Earth fades at her approach.   To rural peace,
Fair plenty, and the social joy of cities,
Soon will succeed rage, rapine, devastation,

3

Each

Each cruel horror fanctify'd by names.
O mortals! mortals! when will you, content
With Nature's bounty, that in fuller flow,
Still as your labours open more its fources, —
Abundant gufhes o'er the happy world;
When will you banifh violence, and outrage
To dwell with beafts of prey in woods and deferts?

TITUS.

Never till *Rome* fhall change her conquering maxims.

GALESUS.

Her haughty fpirit now will foar beyond
Its ufual pitch, upborne by *Caius Marcius.*
Stands he not for the confulate?

TITUS.

He did.
But is no more a citizen of *Rome.*

GALESUS.

What mean'ft thou, *Titus?*

TITUS.

Marcius is from *Rome*
Banifh'd for ever.

GALESUS.

O immortal Powers!
On what pretence could they to exile doom
Their wifeft captain, and their braveft foldier?
Nor lefs renown'd for piety, for juftice,
An uncorrupted heart, and pureft manners.

TITUS.

The charge againft him was entirely groundlefs,

L 3   What

What not his enemies themfelves believ'd,
Affecting of tyrannic power in *Rome*.
His real crime was only fome hot words,
Struck from his fiery temper, in the fenate,
Againft thofe factious minifters of difcord,
The tribunes of the people.   They to rage,
And frantic fury, rous'd the mad plebeians ;
By whom fupported in their bold attempt,
They durft prefume to fummon to the bar
Of an enrag'd and partial populace,
The moft illuftrious fenator of *Rome*.
To this the nobles yielded—and, with his,
Gave up their own and childrens rights for ever.

GALESUS.

O fhameful weaknefs in a *Roman* fenate,
So much renown'd for firmnefs ! yet my *Titus*,
Spite of my love to *Marcius*, I muft own it,
The vigorous foil whence his heroic virtues
Luxuriant rife, if not with careful hand
Severely weeded, teems with imperfections.
His lofty fpirit brooks no oppofition.
His rage, if once offended, knows no bounds.
He deems plebeians, with patrician blood
Compar'd, the creatures of a lower fpecies,
Mere menial hands by Nature meant to ferve him.

TITUS.

It was this high patrician pride undid him.
The furious people triumph'd in his ruin
As if they had expell'd another *Tarquin :*

While,

While, like a captive train, the vanquish'd nobles
Hung their dejected heads in silent shame.
Marcius alone seem'd unconcern'd ; tho' deep
The latent tempest boil'd within his breast,
Choak'd up and smother'd with excessive rage.

GALESUS.

You were his guest at *Rome*, and therefore, *Titus*,
Might on this sad occasion be permitted
To join your tears with his domestic friends.
Saw you that moving scene ?

TITUS.

I did, *Galesus*.

I follow'd *Marcius* home—His mother, there,
Veturia, the most venerable matron
These eyes have e'er beheld, and soft *Volumnia*,
His lovely virtuous wife amidst his children,
Spread on the ground, lay lost in dumb despair.
He swelling stood a while, and could not speak,
Th' affronted hero struggling with the man ;
Then thus at last he broke the gloomy silence ;
" 'Tis done.   The guilty sentence is pronounc'd.
" Ungrateful *Rome* has cast me from her bosom.
" Support this blow with fortitude and courage,
" As it becomes two generous *Roman* matrons.
" I recommend my children to your care.
" Farewel.   I go, I quit, without regret,
" A city grown an enemy to virtue."

GALESUS.

Oh godlike *Marcius !* oh unconquer'd strength

L 4

And

And dignity of mind! How much fuperior
Is fuch a foul to all the power of Fortune!

TITUS.

This faid, he fternly try'd to break away:
When, holding in his hand his eldeft fon,
Vitaria follow'd; while the poor *Volumnia*,
All drown'd in tears, and bearing in one arm
Their youngeft, yet an infant, with the other
Hung clinging at his knees—he, turning to them,
Half foften'd, half fevere, breath'd from his foul
Thefe broken accents—"Ceafe your vain complaints,
" Mother, you have no more a fon; and thou,
" Thou beft of women! thou, my dear *Volumnia!*
" No more a hufband."—Pierc'd with thefe dire words
Volumnia lifelefs funk: and off he flung,
With wild precipitation.

GALESUS.

Thy fad tale
Blinds my old eyes with tears—But whither, tell me,
O whither, *Titus*, bent he then his courfe?

TITUS.

Where the blind genius of regardlefs rage
And defperation led. On to the gate
Capena call'd, attended by the nobles,
He ftalk'd in fullen majefty along;
Nor deign'd a word. A godlike virtuous anger
Beam'd thro' his features, and fublim'd his air.
With downcaft eyes he walk'd; or, if afide
He chanc'd to look, each look was great reproach.

Thus

Thus in emphatic filence, that made words
Void and infipid all, he parted from them,
The day preceding my return from *Rome*;
Nor has been heard of fince, loft in th' abyfs
Of his own woes.

GALESUS.

    O *Marcius*, noble *Marcius*!
How fhall my friendfhip fuccour thy diftrefs?
Where fhall I find thee, to partake thy forrows,
And make myfelf companion of thy exile?
 But, *Titus*, we indulge difcourfe too long—
Go, and affemble thou the *Volfcian* chiefs,
Whilft I repair to *Tullus*, to inform,
And bring him to the council, there to hear
The fatal anfwer thou haft brought from *Rome*.

SCENE II.

Changes to TULLUS's *Tent.*

CORIOLANUS, TULLUS.

CORIOLANUS.

Forgive me, *Tullus*, if I count the moments
That ftop the purpofe of thy noble kindnefs,
And keep me here confin'd in tame inaction.
Why lingers *Titus*?

L 5   TULLUS.

TULLUS.

Calm thy reſtleſs heart,
Brave *Marcius*; every minute I expeᴄt him.
Soon from the cloud that hides thee, ſhalt thou break
With double brightneſs; ſoon thy fiery rage
Shall wither all the ſtrength and pride of *Rome*.

CORIOLANUS.

O righteous *Jove*, proteᴄtor of the injur'd !
If from my earlieſt youth, with pious awe,
I ſtill have reverenc'd thy all-powerful juſtice,
Still by her ſacred diᴄtates rul'd my aᴄtions;
O let that juſtice now ſupport my cauſe,
And arm my ſtrong right-hand with all her terrors !
When that is done, be life or death my lot,
As thy almighty pleaſure ſhall determine.

[*Enter an* Officer *to* Tullus.

OFFICER.

My lord, *Galeſus* aſks admittance to you.

TULLUS.

Marcius, retire an inſtant, till I hear
The buſineſs brings him hither—Bid him enter.

[*Exit* Officer *and* Coriolanus.

[*Enter* Galeſus.

SCENE

SCENE III.

TULLUS, GALESUS.

GALESUS.

Tullus, the *Roman* senate has return'd
No other answer, to our late demands,
But absolute denial and defiance.

TULLUS.

It is what I expected—We shall teach them
An humbler language soon—Hast thou assembled,
As I desir'd, the *Volscian* chiefs in council?

GALESUS.

Titus is gone to summon their attendance.

TULLUS.

It is enough—Come forth, my noble guest!
And shew *Galesus* how the gods assist us.

SCENE IV.

CORIOLANUS, TULLUS, GALESUS.

GALESUS.

O my astonish'd soul; what do I see?
What! *Caius Marcius! Caius Marcius* here,
Beneath one tent with *Tullus?*

L 6

TULLUS.

Ay, and more,
With *Tullus*, now his friend and fellow-foldier.
Yes, thou fhalt fee him thundering at the head
Of *Volfcian* armies, he, who oft has carry'd
Deftruction thro' their ranks—Your leave a moment,
While to our chiefs, and fathers, I announce
Their unexpected gueft.

SCENE V.

CORIOLANUS, GALESUS.

CORIOLANUS.

Thou good old man!
Clofe let me ftrain thee to my faithful heart,
Which now is doubly thine, united more
By the protection which thy country gives me,
Than by our former friendfhip.

GALESUS.

Strange event!
This is thy work, almighty Providence!
Whofe power, beyond the ftretch of human thought,
Revolves the orbs of empire; bids them fink
Deep in the deadning night of thy difpleafure,
Or rife majeftic o'er a wondering world.
The gods by thee—I fee it, *Coriolanus*,—
Mean to exalt us, and deprefs the *Romans*.

CORIO-

CORIOLANUS.

Galesus, yes, the gods have sent me hither;
Those righteous gods, who, when vindictive justice
Excites them to destroy a worthless people,
Make their own crimes and follies strike the blow.

GALESUS.

Cherish these thoughts, that teach us what we are,
And tame the pride of man.   There is a power
Unseen that rules th' illimitable world,
That guides its motions, from the brightest star,
To the least dust of this sin-tainted mold;
While man, who madly deems himself the lord
Of all, is nought but weakness and dependance.
This sacred truth, by sure experience taught,
Thou must have learnt, when, wandering all alone,
Each bird, each insect, flitting thro' the sky,
Was more sufficient for itself, than thou ——
Ah the full image of thy woes dissolves me!
The pangs that must have torn, at parting from thee,
Thy mother and thy wife.   I cannot think
Of that sad scene, without some drops of pity!

CORIOLANUS.

Who was it forc'd me to that bitter parting?
Who, in one cruel, hasty moment, chas'd me
From wife, from children, friends, and houshold gods,
Me! who so often had protected theirs?
Who, from the sacred city of my fathers,
Drove me with Nature's commoners to dwell,
To lodge beneath their wide unsheltered roof,
And at their table feed? O blast me, gods!

With

With ev'ry woe! debility of mind,
Dishonour, just contempt, and palsy'd weaknefs,
If I forgive the villains! yes, *Galesus*,
Yes, I will offer to the Powers of vengeance
A great, a glorious victim—a whole city!——
Why, *Tullus*, this delay?

GALESUS.

May *Coriolanus*
Be to the *Volscian* nation, and himself,
The dread, the godlike instrument of justice!
But let not rage and vengeance mix their rancour;
Let them not trouble with their fretful storm,
Their angry gleams, that azure, where enthron'd.
The calm divinity of Justice fits,
And pities, while she punishes, mankind.

CORIOLANUS.

What faidst thou? What, against the Powers of
vengeance?
The gods gave honest Anger, just Revenge,
To be the awful guardians of the rights
And native dignity of human kind.
O were it not for them, the faucy world
Would grow a noisome nest of little tyrants!
Each carrion crow, on eagle merit perch'd,
Would peck his eyes out, and the mungril cur
At pleasure bait the lion—No, *Galesus*,
I would not rashly, nor on light occasion,
Receive the deep impreffion in my breast;
But when the base, the brutal and unjust,

O-

Or worfe than all, th' ungrateful, ftamp it there ;
O I will then, with luxury fupreme,
Enjoy the pleafure of offended gods,
A righteous, juft revenge !—Behold my foul.

[Enter an Officer.

OFFICER.

My lords, th' affembled chiefs defire your prefence.

GALESUS.

Come, noble *Marcius* ; let my joyful hand
Conduct thee thither—Doubt not thy reception
Will be proportion'd to thy fame and merit.

SCENE VI.

The back-fcene opens, and difcovers the deputies of the
  Volfcian *States, affembled in council.* They rife and
  falute Coriolanus ; *then refume their places.*

GALESUS, TULLUS, CORIOLANUS, Senators.

GALESUS.

Affembled ftates, and captains of the *Volfci*,
Behold the chief fo much renown'd in war ;
Our once fo formidable foe, but now
Our proffer'd friend and foldier—*Caius Marcius.*

1ft SENATOR.

We give him hearty welcome from our fouls.

CORIO-

CORIOLANUS.

Most noble chiefs, and fathers of the *Volsci*,
I need not say, how by the people's rage,
And the poor weakness of the timid nobles,
I am expell'd from *Rome*. Had I confin'd
My wishes merely to a safe retreat,
Some *Latine* city might have given me that;
Or any nameless corner. What imports it,
Where a tame patient exile rots in silence?
But, *Volscian* lords, permit me to declare,
I would at once cut short my useless days,
Rather than be that despicable wretch,
Who neither can take vengeance on his foes,
Nor serve his friends. That is my temper, chiefs.
I shall be glad to merit, by my sword,
Th' asylum which I seek among the *Volsci*.
Rome is our common foe: Then let us join
Our common sufferings, passions, and resentments.
Yes, tho' but one, I bring so many wrongs,
So large a share of powerful enmity,
Into the war, as gives me the presumption,
To offer to the *Volscian* states th' alliance
Even of my single arm.——

TULLUS.

That single arm
Is in itself a numerous army, *Marcius*;
The *Volscians* so esteem it—But proceed.

CORIOLANUS.

I will not mention, *Volscian* chiefs, what talent

The

The world allows me to poffefs in war:
But be that what it will, you may employ it.
Soldier, or captain, in whatever ftation
You place me, I will lofe each drop of blood,
Or with this hand I'll fix the *Volfcian* ftandard
On the proud towers of capitolian *Jove.*

Tullus.

Chiefs of the *Volfcian* league I give you joy
Of our new citizen, the noble *Marcius.*
The genius of the *Volfcian* ftate has fent him,
Whetted by wrongs into à keener hatred
Than that we bear to *Rome.*   It were contemning,
With impious felf-fufficient arrogance
This bounty of the gods, not to accept,
With every mark of honour, of his fervice.
I, *Volfcians*, I, even *Attius Tullus*, give,
Firft of you all, my voice, that *Caius Marcius*
Be now receiv'd to high command among us;
That inftantly we do appoint him general
Of half our troops, which here, with your confent,
I to him yield.— Speak, chiefs, is this your pleafure?

1ft Senator.

It is,—We give unanimous confent.

Tullus, *embracing him.*

Marcius, I joy to call thee my companion,
And collegue in this war.

Coriolanus.

                By all the gods!
Thou art the generous victor of my foul!

Yes, *Tullus*, I am conquer'd by thy virtue.

GALESUS.

Tho' I have oft, on great occasions, *Tullus*,
Beheld thee in the senate, and the field,
Cover'd with glory ; yet, I must avow,
I never saw thee shew such genuine greatness,
Such true sublimity of soul, as now.
To scorn th' all-powerful charm of selfish passions,
Chiefly the dazzling pride of emulation,
That noble weakness of heroic minds,
To sink thyself that thou may'st raise thy country ;
To put the sword into thy rival's hand,
And twine thy promis'd laurels round his brow——
O 'tis a flight beyond the highest point
Of martial glory ! and what few can reach.
Go forth, ye chosen ministers of justice ;
And may that awful Power, whose secret hand
Sways all our passions, turns our partial views.
All to its own dread purposes, attend you !

CORIOLANUS.

I burn to enter on the glorious task
You now have mark'd me out.   How slow the times
To the warm soul, that, in the very instant
It forms, would execute, a great design.
'Tis my advice we march direct to *Rome* ;
We cannot be too quick.   Let the first dawn
See us in bright array before her walls.
Perhaps when they behold their exile there,
Back'd by your force, some conscious hearts among
            them

                                        May

May feel th' alarm of guilt.

TULLUS.

I much approve
Of this advice. 'Tis what I thought before,
Ere ftrengthen'd, *Marcius*, by thy mighty arm :
But now 'tis doubly right. Here, *Volfcian* chiefs,
Here let our council terminate—The troops
Have had repofe fufficient. Strait to *Rome*
Come, let us urge our march—As yet the ftars
Ride in their middle watch ; we fhall with eafe,
Reach it by dawn——

CORIOLANUS.

Yes, we have time—too much !
Six tedious hours till morn—But hence ! away !
My foul on fire anticipates the dawn.

The End of the Second Act.

ACT III. SCENE I.

CORIOLANUS.

NO more—I merit not this lavish praise.
True, we have driven the *Roman* legions back,
Defeated, and difgrac'd—But what is this?
Nothing, ye *Volfci*, nothing yet is done.
We but begin the wonderous leaf of ftory,
That marks the *Roman* doom. At length it dawns,
The deftin'd hour, that eafes of their fears
The nations round, and fets *Hefperia* free.
Come on, my brave companions of the war!
Come, let us finifh at one mighty ftroke
This toil of labouring fate.—We will, or perifh!
While, noble *Tullus*, you protect the camp,
I, with my troops, all men of chofen valour,
And well-approv'd to-day, will ftorm the city.

TITUS.

Beneath thy animating conduct, *Marcius*,

What

What can the *Volscian* valour not perform?
Thy very fight and voice fubdues the *Romans*.
When, lifting up your helm, you fhew'd your face,
That like a comet glar'd deftruction on them,
I faw their braveft veterans fly before thee.
Their ancient fpirit has with thee forfook them,
And ruin hangs o'er yon devoted walls.

[*Enter an* Officer, *who addreffes himfelf
to* Coriolanus.

OFFICER.

My lord, a herald is arriv'd from *Rome*,
To fay, a deputation from the fenate,
Attended by the minifters of Heaven,
A venerable train of priefts and flamens,
Is on the way, addrefs'd to you.

CORIOLANUS.

To me!
What can this meffage mean!—Stand to your arms,
Ye *Volfcian* troops; and let thefe *Romans* pafs
Betwixt the lowring frown of double files.
What! do they think me fuch a milky boy,
To pay my vengeance with a few foft words.
Come, fellow foldiers, *Tullus*, come, and fee,
If I betray the honours you have done me.

[*Goes out with a train of* Volfcian *officers.*

SCENE

SCENE II.

TULLUS, VOLUSIUS, *who remain.*

VOLUSIUS, *after some silence.*
Are we not, *Tullus,* failing in our duty
Not to attend our general?

     TULLUS.
       How! what saidst thou?

VOLUSIUS.
Methought, my lord, his parting orders were,
We should attend the triumph now preparing
O'er all his foes at once—*Romans* and *Volsci!*
Come, we shall give offence.

    TULLUS.
      Of this no more.
I pray thee spare thy bitter irony.

    VOLUSIUS.
Shall I then speak without disguise?

     TULLUS.
        Speak out
With all the honest bluntness of a friend.
Think'st thou I fear the truth?

    VOLUSIUS.
      Then, *Tullus,* know,
Thou art no more the general of the *Volsci.*
Thou hast, by this thy generous weakness, sunk
Thyself into a private man of *Antium.*

          Yes,

Yes, thou haft taken from thy laurel'd brow
The well-earn'd trophies of thy toils and perils,
Thy fpringing hopes, the faireft ever budded,
And heap'd them on a man too proud before.

TULLUS.

He bears it high.

VOLUSIUS.

    Death and perdition! high!
With uncontroul'd command!—You fee, already,
He will not be encumber'd with the fetters
Of our advice. He fpeaks his fovereign will;
On every hand he iffues out his orders,
As to his natural flaves.—For you, my lord,
He has, I think, confin'd you to your camp,
There in inglorious indolence to languifh;
While he, beneath your blafted eyes, fhall reap
The harveft of your honour.

TULLUS.

    No, *Volufius*,
Whatever honour fhall by him be gain'd
Reverts to me, from whofe fuperior bounty
He drew the means of all his glorious deeds.
This mighty chief, this conqueror of *Rome*
Is but my creature.——

VOLUSIUS.

    Wretched felf-delufion;
He and the *Volfcians* know he is thy mafter.
He acts as fuch in all things.—Now by *Mars*,
Could my abhorrent foul endure the thought

          Of

Of stooping to a *Roman* chief, I here
Would leave thee in thy solitary camp,
And go where glory calls.

TULLUS.

Indeed, *Volusius*,
I did expect more equal treatment from him.
But what of that ?—The generous pride of virtue
Disdains to weigh too nicely the returns
Her bounty meets with—Like the liberal gods,
From her own gracious nature she bestows,
Nor stoops to ask reward—Yet must I own,
I thought he would not have so soon forgot
What he so lately was, and what I am.

VOLUSIUS.

Gods ! knew ye not his character before ?
Did you not know his genius was to yours
Averse, as are antipathies in nature ?
High, over-weening, tyrannously proud,
And only fit to hold command o'er slaves ?
Hence, as repugnant to that equal life,
Which is the quickening soul of all republics,
The *Roman* people cast him forth ; and we,
Shall we receive the bane of their repose,
Into our breast ? Are we less free than they ?
Or shall we be more patient of a tyrant ?

TULLUS.

All this I knew. But while his imperfections
Are thy glad theme, thou hast forgot his virtues.

VOLU-

VOLUSIUS.

I leave that fubject to the fmooth *Galefus*,
And thefe his *Volfcian* flatterers—His virtues!
Truft me there is no infolence that treads
So high as that which rears itfelf on virtue.

TULLUS.

Well, be it fo—I meant, that even his vices
Should, on this great occafion, ferve the *Volfci*.

VOLUSIUS.

Confufion! there it is! there lurks the fting
Of our difhonour! while this *Marcius* leads
The *Roman* armies, ours are driven before him.
Behold, he changes fides; when with him changes
The fortune of the war. Strait they grow *Volfci*
And we victorious *Romans*—Such, no doubt,
Such is his fecret boaft—Ay, this vile brand
Succefs itfelf will fix for ever on us;
And, *Tullus*, thou, 'tis thou muft anfwer for it.

TULLUS *afide*.

His words are daggers to my heart; I feel
Their truth, but am afham'd to own my folly.

VOLUSIUS.

O fhame! O infamy! the thought confumes me,
It fcalds my eyes with tears, to fee a *Roman*
Borne on our fhoulders to immortal fame:
Juft in the happy moment that decided
The long difpute of ages, that for which
Our generous anceftors had toil'd and bled,
To fee him then ftep in and fteal our glory!

VOL. IV. M *O that*

O that we firſt had periſh'd all ! A people,
Who cannot find in their own proper force
Their own protection, are not worth the ſaving !

TULLUS.

It muſt have way ! I will no more ſuppreſs it—
    Know then, my rough old friend, no leſs than thee
His conduct hurts me and upbraids my folly.
I wake as from a dream.   What demon mov'd me?
What doating generoſity ? his woes,
Was it his woes ! To ſee the brave reduc'd
To truſt his mortal foe ? perhaps, a little
That work'd within my boſom—But, *Voluſius*,
That was not all—I will to thee confeſs
The weakneſs of my heart—Yes, it was pride,
The dazzling pride to ſee my rival-warrior
The great *Coriolanus*, bend his ſoul,
His haughty ſoul, to ſue for my protection.
Protection ſaid I ? were it that alone,
I had been baſe to have refus'd him that,
To have refus'd him aught a gallant foe
Owes to a gallant foe.—But to exalt him
To the ſame level, nay, above myſelf;
To yield him the command of half my troops,
The choiceſt acting half—That, that was madneſs !
Was weak, was mean, unworthy of a man !——

VOLUSIUS.

I ſcorn to flatter thee—It was indeed.

TULLUS.

Curſe on the ſlave *Galeſus !* ſoothing, he

I   Seiz'd

Seiz'd the fond moment of infatuation,
And clinch'd the chains my generous folly forg'd.
How shall I from this labyrinth escape?
Must it then be! what cruel genius dooms me,
In war or peace to creep beneath his fortune?

VOLUSIUS.

That genius is thyself. If thou canst bear
The very thought of stooping to this *Roman*,
Thou from that moment art his vassal, *Tullus*;
By that thou dost acknowledge, parent Nature
Has form'd him thy superior. But if fix'd
Upon the base of manly resolution,
Thou say'st—I will be free! I will command!
I and my country! then—O never doubt it—
We shall find means to crush this vain intruder;
Even I myself—this hand——
     Nay, hear me, *Tullus*,
'Tis not yet come to that, that last resource.
I do not say we should employ the dagger,
While other, better means are in our power.

TULLUS.

No, my *Volusius*, Fortune will not drive us,
Or I am much deceiv'd, to that extreme;
We shall not want the strongest fairest plea,
To give a solemn sanction to his fate.
He will betray himself. Whate'er his rage
Of passion talks, a weakness for his country
Sticks in his soul, and he is still a *Roman*.
Soon shall we see him tempted to the brink

Of this fure precipice—Then down, at once,
Without remorfe, we hurl him to perdition!
    But hark! the trumpet calls us to a fcene
I fhould deteft, if not from hope we thence
May gather matter to mature our purpofe.

SCENE III.

The back-fcene opens, and difcovers Coriolanus *fitting on his tribunal, attended by his lictors, and a croud of* Volfcian *officers. Files of troops drawn up on either hand. In the depth of the fcene appear the deputies from the* Roman *fenate,* M. Minucius, Pofthumus Cominius, Sp. Lartius, P. Pinnarius, *and* Q. Sulpitius, *all confular fenators, who had been his moft zealous friends And behind them march the priefts, the facrificers, the augurs, and the guardians of the facred things, dreft in their ceremonial habits. Thefe advance flowly betwixt the files of foldiers, under arms. As* Tullus *enters,* Coriolanus *rifing falutes him.*

CORIOLANUS.

Here, noble *Tullus*, fit, and judge my conduct;
Nor fpare to check me, if I act amifs.

                TULLUS.

TULLUS.

Marcius, the *Volscian* fate is in thy hands.

[*Coriolanus is seated again, and* Tullus *places himself upon a tribunal on his left hand. Mean time the* Roman *deputies advance up to* Coriolanus *and salute him, which he returns.*

CORIOLANUS.

What, *Romans*, from the generals of the *Volsci*
Is your demand?

MINUCIUS.

O *Coriolanus*, *Rome*,
Nurse of thy tender years, thy parent-city,
Her senators, her people, priests, and augurs,
Her every order and degree, by us,
Thy ever-zealous, still unshaken friends,
Sue in the most pathetic terms for peace.
And if in this constrain'd, we from our maxim,
Never to ask but give it, must depart; .
It is some consolation, in the state
To which thou hast by thy superior valour
Reduc'd us, that we ask it from a *Roman*.

CORIOLANUS.

I was a *Roman* once, and thought the name
Was not dishonour'd by me; but it pleas'd
Your lords, the mob of *Rome*, to take it from me;
Nor will I now receive it back again.

MINUCIUS.

The name thou mayst reject, but canst not throw
The duties from thee which that name imports;

Indis-

Indissoluble duties, bound upon thee
By the strong hand of Nature, and confirm'd
By the dread sanction of all-ruling *Jove*.
Then hear thy country's supplicating voice;
By all those duties I conjure thee hear us.

CORIOLANUS.

Well—I will hear thee; speak, declare thy message.

MINUCIUS.

Give peace, give healing peace, to two brave nations,
Fatigu'd with war, and sick of cruel deeds!
To carry on destruction's easy trade,
Afflict mankind, and scourge the world with war,
Is what each wicked, each ambitious man,
Who lets his furious passions loose, may do:
But in the flattering torrent of success,
To check his rage, and drop th' avenging sword,
When a repenting people ask it of him,
That is the genuine bounty of a god.
Then urge no farther this your just resentment;
Which, injur'd as you are, you needs must feel,
But never ought to carry into action,
Against your sacred country; whence you drew
Your life, your virtues, every mortal good,
That very valour you employ against her.
Stop, *Coriolanus*, ere, beyond retreat,
You plunge yourself in crimes.   To the fierce joy
Of vengeance push'd to barbarous excess,
Repentance will succeed, and sickning horror.
Consider too the slippery state of fortune.

The

The gods take pleasure oft, when haughty mortals
On their own pride erect a mighty fabric,
By slightest means, to lay their towering schemes
Low in the dust, and teach them they are nothing.
Return, thou virtuous *Roman!* to the bosom
Of thy imploring country. Lo! her arms
She fondly spreads to take thee back again,
And by redoubled love efface her harshness.
Return, and crown thee with the noblest wreathe
Which glory can bestow—the palm of mercy!

CORIOLANUS.

Marcus Minucius, and ye other *Romans*,
Respected senators, and holy flamens,
Attend, and take to your demand this answer:
  Why court you me, the servant of the *Volsci?*
It is to them that you must bend for peace,
Which on these only terms they will accord you.
" Restore the conquer'd lands, your former wars
" Have ravish'd from them: from their towns and
      cities,
" Won by your arms, withdraw your colonics;
" And to the full immunities of *Rome*
" Frankly admit them, as you have the *Latines*."
Then, *Romans*, ye have peace, and not till then!
If these are terms which suit not your ambition,
They suit the state to which the *Volscian* arms
Have now reduc'd you—We have learn'd from *Rome*
To use our fortune, and command the vanquish'd.

TULLUS *aside*.

Death to my hopes! I'm now his slave for ever.

CORIO.

CORIOLANUS, *addreſſing himſelf to the* Volſci.

This, my illuſtrious patrons and protectors,
Volſci, to you I ow'd.   Permit me now
To do myſelf and injur'd honour-juſtice.

               [*Turning again to the* Romans.

As to the liberty you idly vaunt
To give me of returning to your city,
'Tis what I hold unworthy of acceptance.
Can I return into th' ungrateful boſom
Of a diſtracted ſtate, where, to the rage
Of a vile ſenſeleſs populace, the laws
Are by your ſhameful weakneſs given a prey?
Who are the men that hold the ſway among you?
And whom have you expell'd, as even unworthy
To live within the cincture of your walls!—
O the wild thought breaks in and troubles reaſon!—
With what, ye *Romans*, can the ſowereſt cenſor,
The moſt envenom'd malice, juſtly charge me?
Did I e'er break your laws? Nay, did I e'er
Do aught that could diſturb the ſacred order,
The peace and ſocial harmony of life;
Or taint your ancient ſanctity of manners?
What was my crime? I could not bear to ſee
Your dignity debas'd, to ſee the rabble
Tread on the reverend grey authority
Of ſenatorial wiſdom: Yes, for you,
In your defence I did enrage this monſter;
And yet you baſely left me to its fury.
Then talk no more of ſervices and friendſhip:
                      A friend,

A friend, who can, and does not shield, betrays me.
Or if the power was wanting, then your senate
Is sunk into servility and bondage,
Nor should a freeman deign to sit among you.

MINUCIUS.

The wiseft are sometimes compell'd to yield
To popular ftorms : yet I defend not, *Marcius*,
Our timid conduct ; we have felt our error,
And now invite thee back to aid the fenate,
With thy heroic fpirit to reftrain
The giddy rage of faction, and to hold
The reins of government more firm hereafter.

As to th' appeal which thou haft nobly made
In vindication of thy fpotlefs fame,
With pleafure we confirm it, and bear witnefs
To all thy public and thy private virtues :
But let us alfo beg thee not to ftain
The brightnefs of that glory by a crime,
Which, unrepented, would difgrace them all,
A dire rebellious war againft thy country.

CORIOLANUS.

Abfurd ! what can you mean ? To call a people,
Who with the laft indignity have us'd me,
To call my foes my country ! No, *Minucius*,
It is the generous nation of the *Volfci*.
Thefe brave, thefe virtuous men, you fee around me,
Who, when I wander'd a poor helplefs exile,
Took pity of my injuries and woes ;
Forgot the former mifchiefs of my fword ;

Heap'd on me kindnefs, honours, dignities;
Fear'd not to truft me with this high command,
And plac'd me here the guardian of their caufe:——
Be witnefs, *Jove!*—It is alone their nation
I henceforth will acknowledge for my country!
Let this fuffice—You have my anfwer, *Romans*.

COMINIUS.

This anfwer, *Coriolanus*, is the dictate
More of thy pride than magnanimity:
'Tis thy revenge that gives it, not thy virtue.
Art thou above the gods? who joy to fhow'r
Their doubled goodnefs on repenting mortals?
But think not I intend, by this, to urge
Our proffer'd peace, fo harfhly treated, further.
That were a weaknefs ill becoming *Romans*.
Yet I muft tell thee, it would better fuit
A fierce defpotic chief of barbarous flaves,
Than the calm dignity of one who fits
In the grave fenate of a free republic,
To talk fo high, and as it were to thruft
Plebeians from the native rights of man.——

CORIOLANUS.

Ha! doft thou come the people's advocate
To me, *Cominius!* com'ft thou to infult me!

COMINIUS.

Nay, hear me, *Marcius:*—Thefe grey hairs impower
    me
To fet thee right before this great affembly:
And there was once a time, thou wouldft have heard
                                    Thy

Thy general with more deference and patience—
I tell thee then, whoe'er amidſt the ſons
Of reaſon, valour, liberty, and virtue,
Diſplays diſtinguiſh'd merit, is a noble
Of Nature's own creating.   Such have riſen,
Sprung from the duſt; or where had been our honours?
And ſuch in radiant bands will riſe again,
In yon immortal city, that, when moſt
Depreſs'd by fate, and near apparent ruin,
Returns, as with an energy divine,
On her aſtoniſh'd foes, and ſhakes them from her—
Your pardon, *Volſci*—But this, *Coriolanus*,
Is what I had to ſay.

CORIOLANUS.

And I have heard it—

[Riſing from his tribunal; and the
prieſts advancing to addreſs him,
he prevents them.

For you, ye awful miniſters of Heaven,
Let me not hear your holy lips profan'd
By urging what my duty muſt refuſe.
I bow in adoration to the gods;
I venerate their ſervants.   But there is,
There is a power, their chief, their darling care,
The guardian of mankind, which to betray
Were violating all—And that is Juſtice.
   So far my public character demands;
So far my honour.—Now, what ſhould forbid
The man, and friend, to be indulg'd a little?

M 6

Permit me to embrace thee, good *Minucius*,
Thee, *Lartius* ; you, *Pinnarius* and *Sulpitius* :
But chiefly thee, *Cominius*, who firſt rais'd me
To deeds of arms : who from thy conſular brow
Took thy own crown, and with it circled mine.
Tho' nought can ſhake my purpoſe, yet I wiſh
That *Rome* had ſent me others on this errand.
I thank you for your friendſhip. The protection,
Which you have given to thoſe, whom once I call'd
By tender names, I would not now remember.
How ſhall I—ſay—return your generous goodneſs?
O, there is nothing you, as friends, can aſk,
My grateful heart will not with pleaſure grant you.

COMINIUS.

We thank thee, *Coriolanus*—But a *Roman*
Diſdains that favour you refuſe his country.

CORIOLANUS.

[*To the* Volſcian *officers.*
See that they be, with due regard and ſafety,
Conducted back.

[*To the* Roman *ſenators.*
I will ſuſpend th' aſſault,
Till to theſe terms, of which we will not bate
The ſmalleſt part, your ſenate may have time
To ſend their lateſt anſwer. Then we cut
All further treaty off. *Romans*, farewel.

The End of the Third Act.

A C T

ACT IV. SCENE I.

TULLUS, *alone.*

WHAT is the mind of man ? A reftlefs fcene
    Of vanity and weaknefs ; fhifting ftill,
As fhift the lights of our uncertain knowledge ;
Or as the various gale of paflion breathes.
   None ever thought himfelf more deeply founded ;
On what is right, nor felt a nobler ardor,
Than I, when I invefted *Caius Marcius*
With this ill-judg'd command. Now it appears
Diftraction, folly, monftrous folly ! meannefs !
And down I plunge, betray'd even by my virtue,
From gulph to gulph, from fhame to deeper fhame.

SCENE II.

TULLUS, GALESUS.

GALESUS.

I liften'd, *Tullus*, to th' important fcene
That lately pafs'd before us, with moft ftrict
                    Unpre-

Unprejudic'd attention; and have fince
Revolv'd it in my mind, both as a man,
Ally'd to all mankind, and as a *Volfcian*.
Indeed our terms are high, and by the manner
In which they were prefcrib'd by *Coriolanus*,
Are what we cannot hope will e'er be granted.
They fhould be foften'd. Let us yield a little,
Confcious ourfelves to a great nation's pride,
The pride of human nature. Could the *Romans*
Stoop to fuch peace, commanded by the fword
They then were flaves, unworthy our alliance.

TULLUS.

Gods! do I hear in thee, one of the chiefs
Intrufted with the honour of the *Volfci*,
An advocate for *Rome*?

GALESUS.

I glory, *Tullus*,
To own myfelf an advocate for peace.
Peace is the happy natural ftate of man ;
War his corruption, his difgrace—

TULLUS.

His fafeguard !
His pride ! his glory !—What but war, juft war,
Gave *Greece* her heroes? Thofe who drew the fword
(As we do now) againft the fons of rapine ;
To quell proud tyrants, and to free mankind.

GALESUS.

Yes, *Tullus*, when to juft defence the warrior
Confines his force, he is a worfhip'd name,

Dear

Dear to mankind, the firſt and beſt of mortals!
Yet ſtill, if this can by ſoft means be done,
And fair accommodation, that is better.
Why ſhould we purchaſe with the blood of thouſands,
What may be gain'd by mutual juſt conceſſion?
Why give up peace, the beſt of human bleſſings,
For the vain cruel pride of uſeleſs conqueſt?

TULLUS.

Theſe ſoothing dreams of philoſophic quiet
Are only fit for unfrequented ſhades.
The ſage ſhould quit the buſy buſtling world,
Ill ſuited to his gentle meditations,
And in ſome deſert find that peace he loves.

GALESUS.

Miſtaken man! Philoſophy conſiſts not
In airy ſchemes, or idle ſpeculations:
The rule and conduct of all ſocial life
Is her great province. Not in lonely cells
Obſcure ſhe lurks, but holds her heavenly light
To ſenates and to kings, to guide their councils,
And teach them to reform and bleſs mankind.
All policy but her's is falſe and rotten;
All valour not conducted by her precepts
Is a deſtroying fury ſent from hell
To plague unhappy man, and ruin nations.

TULLUS.

To ſtop the waſte of that deſtroying fury
Is the great cauſe and purpoſe of this war.
Art thou a friend to peace?—ſubdue the *Romans*.

Who,

Who, who, but they, have turn'd this ancient land,
Where, from *Saturnian* times, harmonious concord
Still lov'd to dwell, into a scene of blood,
Of endless discord, and perpetual rapine ?
The sword, the vengeful sword, must drain away
This boiling blood, that thus disturbs the nations !
Talk not of terms. It is a vain attempt
To bind th' ambitious and unjust by treaties :
These they elude a thousand specious ways ;
Or if they cannot find a fair pretext,
They blush not in the face of Heaven to break them.

GALESUS.

Why then affronted Heaven will combat for us.
Set justice on our side, and then my voice
Shall be as loud for war as thine ; my sword
Shall strike as deep ; at least my blood shall flow
As freely, *Tullus*, in my country's cause.
But as I then would die to serve the *Volscians*,
So now I dare to serve them by opposing,
Even with my single voice, th' impetuous torrent
That hurries us away beyond the bounds
Of temperate wisdom ; and presume to tell thee,
It is thy passion, not thy prudence dictates
This haughty language.

TULLUS.

Yes, it is my passion,
A passion for the glory of my country,
That scorns your narrow views of timid prudence.
Our injur'd honour drew our swords, and never

Shall

Shall they be fheath'd while I command the *Volfcians*,.
Till *Rome* fubmits to *Antium*.

GALESUS.

Rome will perifh
Ere fhe fubmit; and fhe has ftill her walls,
The ftrength of her allies, her native valour,
Which oft has fav'd her in the worft extremes,
And, ftronger yet than all, defpair, to aid her.

TULLUS.

All thefe will nought avail her, if our fears
Come not to her affiftance—But, *Galefus*,
Why urge you this to me? Go, talk to *Marcius*.
The war has given him all his pride could hope for,
To fee *Rome*'s fenate humbled at his feet:
He now may wifh to reign in peace at *Antium*,
And thou, perhaps, art come an envoy from him,.
To learn if I fhall prove a quiet fubject.

GALESUS.

Thro' this unguarded opening of thy foul,
I fee what ftings thee—Ah! beware of envy!
If that pale fury feize thee, thou art loft!
Tullus, 'tis eafier far, from the clear breaft,
To keep out treacherous vice, than to expel it.
Farewel. Remember I have done my duty.

[*Goes out*.

TULLUS, *alone*.

This man difcerns my heart—Well: What of that?
Am I afraid its movements fhould be feen?
I, whofe clear thoughts have never fhunn'd the light,

Muft

Muſt I now ſeek to hide them ? O misfortune !
To have reduc'd myſelf to ſuch a ſtate,
So much beneath the greatneſs of my ſoul,
That, like a coward, I muſt learn to praƈtiſe
The wretched arts of vile diſſimulation !
By Heaven, I will not do it—I will not ſtoop
To veil my diſcontent a moment longer.
But ſee ! my rival comes, the happy *Marcius.*
His haughty mien, his very looks, affront me.

SCENE III.

CORIOLANUS, TULLUS.

CORIOLANUS.

Tullus, I have receiv'd intelligence,
That a ſtrong body of the *Latin* troops
Is in full march to raiſe the ſiege of *Rome.*
Another day will bring them to its aid.
But go thou forth, and lead the valiant bands,
By thee commanded, to repel theſe ſuccours.
Go, and cut off from *Rome* its laſt reſource.

TULLUS.

I lead my troops, from the great ſcene of aƈtion,
From falling *Rome,* which, ere to-morrow's ſun
Shall ſet, may be our prey ! ſure you forget
My rank and ſtation—I diſdain the ſervice :
Give it to ſome you may command.   For me,

I own

I own no mafter but the *Volfcian* ftates.
Rome is my object. I from *Antium* brought
The nobleft army ever fhook her walls.
And fhall I now, on that decifive day,
Doom'd by the gods to lay her pride in afhes,
Shall I be abfent from the glorious work?
It is the higheft outrage even to think it.—
Juft gods! doft thou prefume to give thy orders
To me? to me! thy equal in command?
Nay, thy fuperior? was it not my'hand,
My lavifh hand, beftow'd thy power upon thee?
And know, proud *Roman*, that the man who gave it,
Can at his will refume it.

CORIOLANUS.

     I propos'd
This expedition to thee as thy friend,
Not as thy general, *Tullus.* We are both
Commanders here; and for my fhare of pow'r,
Whene'er the council of the *Volfcian* ftates,
Who cloath'd me with it, fhall again demand it,
I at their feet will lay it down, perfuaded,
The canker'd tongue of Envy's felf muft own,
That by my fervice I have well deferv'd it.

TULLUS.

Was it to them, or me, you hither came
To crave protection? Was not then your fortune,
Your liberty, your life, at my difpofal?
I rais'd you from the duft, a wretched exile,
An outcaft, helplefs, friendlefs, driven to beg,
          The

The lowest refuge which despair can seek,
Shelter amidst thy foes.   My pitying goodness
Protected, trusted, and believ'd'you grateful.
O ill-plac'd confidence!——

CORIOLANUS.

Immortal gods !
Hear I these words from *Tullus !*

TULLUS.

What for all this
Is thy return ? Pride; self-sufficiency ;
Councils apart from mine ; despotic orders ;
The glory of the war all pilfer'd from me :
And, to complete the whole, a *Latin* army
Now conjur'd up to draw me from the siege ;
Till by cajoling our tame chiefs, and dazzling
The senseless eyes of the low mob of soldiers,
Thou shalt be solely seated in the power
Which, thank my folly! now is shar'd betwixt us.

CORIOLANUS.

O indignation !—Down, thou swelling heart—
I will be calm—I will.—Thou dost accuse me
Of the worst vice that can debase mankind,
Of black ingratitude.   On what foundations ?
What have I done to merit such a charge ?
Is it my fault, if in the *Volscian* army
My name is as rever'd and great as thine ?
Can I forbid authority, and fame,
To follow merit and success ?—You knew
The man whom you employ'd, and should have known
He

He would not be a cypher in employment.

TULLUS.

Think'ft thou my heart can better brook than thine
To be that cypher! that diſhonour'd tool!
Subfervient to th' ambition of another?
Gods! I had rather live a drudging peafant,
Unknown to glory, in fome *Alpin* village;
Than at the head of thefe victorious legions,
Bear the high name of chief, without the power,
No, *Marcius*, no.   I will command indeed:
And thou ſhalt learn, with all the *Volfcian* army
To treat their general with refpect.

CORIOLANUS.

Refpect!

O *Tullus! Tullus!* by the Powers divine!
I bore thee once refpect, as high as man
Can ſhew to man.   From thee, my foe, my rival,
I nor difdain'd nor fear'd to afk protection.
You gave me all I afk'd, you gave me more,
With noble warmth of heart! which to efteem,
Added the ties of gratitude, and friendſhip.
Whatever fince, in council, or in arms,
Has been by me atchiev'd, was done for thee.
My glory all was thine.   The palms I gain'd
Only compos'd a garland for his brow,
Who rais'd this banifh'd man to tread on *Rome*.

TULLUS.

To tread on him who rais'd him—That, I know,
Is thy ambitious purpofe; but be certain,

However

However *Rome* may bend beneath thy fortune,
Thou shalt not find an easy conquest here.

CORIOLANUS.

May *Jove* with lightning strike me to the centre,
If from the day I saw thy face at *Antium*,
My heart has ever form'd one secret thought
To hurt thy honour, or depress thy greatness:
I was thy friend, thy soldier, and thy servant.
But now I will as openly avow,
Thy jealousy has, with envenom'd breath,
Made such a sudden ravage in our friendship,
I know not what to think.——

TULLUS.

Think me thy foe.
There is no lasting friendship with the proud.

CORIOLANUS.

Nor with the jealous——But of this enough.
Come, let us turn our fire a nobler way:
We have a worthier quarrel to pursue.——
It were unjust, dishonourable, base,
Our pride should hurt the *Volscian* cause.

TULLUS.

No, *Marcius*,
I mean to guard it better for the future:
The *Volscian* cause is safest with a *Volscian*.
I therefore claim, insist upon my right;
That you shall yield me my command in turn.
The first attack was yours: 'Tis scanty justice,
The second should be mine.

CORI-

CORIOLANUS.

Tullus, 'tis yours.
O it imports not which of us command!
Give me the loweſt rank among your troops:
All *Italy* will know, the voice of fame
Will tell all future times, that I was preſent;
That *Coriolanus* in the *Volſcian* army
Aſſiſted, when imperial *Rome* was ſack'd;
That city which, while he maintain'd her cauſe,
Invincible herſelf, made *Antium* tremble.

TULLUS.

What arrogant preſumption!

SCENE IV.

To them VOLUSIUS, *entering haſtily.*

TULLUS.

Ha! *Voluſius*,
Thy looks declare ſome meſſage of importance.

VOLUSIUS.

Tullus, they do—I was to find thee, *Marcius*.
To thee a ſecond deputation comes,
Thy mother, and thy wife, with a long train
Of all the nobleſt ladies *Rome* can boaſt,
In mourning habits clad, approach our camp,
Preceded by a herald, to demand
Another audience of thee.

CORIO-

CORIOLANUS.

How, *Volusius !*

Said you, the *Roman* ladies! Low, indeed,
Must be the state of *Rome*, when thus her matrons
She sends amidst the tumults of a camp,
To beg protection for the men, who lie
Trembling behind their ramparts—come! once more!
And see me put an end to prayers and treaty!

SCENE V.

TULLUS, VOLUSIUS.

VOLUSIUS.

Tullus, 'tis well. This answers to my wishes.

TULLUS.

How? What is well? That humbled *Rome* once more
Shall deck him with the trophies of our arms?

VOLUSIUS.

And hop'st thou nothing from this blest event?
They who have often blasted mighty heroes,
Who oft have stoln into the firmest hearts,
And melted them to folly; they, my friend,
Will do what wisdom never could effect.

TULLUS.

Think'st thou the prayers and tears of wailing women
Can shake the man, who with such cold disdain

2   Stood

Stood firm againſt thoſe venerable conſuls,
And ſpurn'd the genius of his kneeling country ?

VOLUSIUS.

It was his pride alone that made him ours.
That paſſion kept him firm ; the flattering charm
Of humbling thoſe, who in their perſons bore
The whole collected majeſty of *Rome*.
Theſe women are no proper objects for it :
He cannot triumph o'er his wife and mother.
On this my hopes are founded, that theſe women
May by their gentler influence ſubdue him.

TULLUS.

Whate'er th' event, he ſhall no longer here,
As wave his paſſions, dictate peace or war.
Whether his ſtubborn ſoul maintains its firmneſs,
Or yields to female prayers, the *Volſcian* honour
Will be alike betray'd. If *Rome* prevails,
He ſtops our conquering arms from her deſtruction ;
If he rejects her ſuit, he reigns our tyrant.
But, by th' immortal gods ! his ſhort-liv'd empire
Shall never ſee yon radiant ſun deſcend.

VOLUSIUS.

Bleſt be thoſe gods that have at laſt inſpir'd thee
With reſolution equal to thy cauſe,
The cauſe of liberty !——

TULLUS.

Be ſure, *Voluſius*,
If that ſhould happen which thy hopes portend ;

Should he, by Nature tam'd. difarm'd by love,
Refpite the *Roman* doom—He feals his own :
By Heaven ! he dies.

VOLUSIUS.

Let me embrace thee, *Tullus !*
Now breaking from the cloud, which, like the fun,
Thy own too bounteous beams had drawn around thee.

TULLUS.

You was deceiv'd, my friend. When I with tamenefs,
With tamenefs which aftonifh'd thy brave fpirit,
Seem'd to fubmit to that unequal fway
He arrogated o'er me ; know, my heart
Ne'er fwell'd fo high as in that cruel moment.
My indignation, like th' imprifon'd fire
Pent in the troubled breaft of glowing *Ætna,*
Burnt deep and filent : But, collected now,
It fhall beneath its fury bury *Marcius !*
'Tis fixt. Our tyrant dies.

VOLUSIUS.

Tullus, my fword
Here claims to be employ'd.—Nor mine alone—
There are fome worthy *Volfci* ftill remaining,
Who think with us. and pine beneath the laurels
A *Roman* chief beftows.

TULIUS.

Go, find them ftrait,
And bring them to the fpace before his tent ;
'Tis there he will receive this deputation.

Then

Then if he finks beneath thefe womens prayers —
Or if he does not — But, *Volufius*, wait,
I give thee ftricteft charge to wait my fignal.
Perhaps I may find means to free the *Volfci*
Without his blood. If not — we will be free.

The End of the Fourth Act.

ACT V. SCENE I.

Trumpets sounding.

The scene discovers the camp, a croud of Volscian *officers with files of soldiers drawn up as before. Enter* Coriolanus, Tullus, Galesus, Volusius. *The* Roman *ladies advance slowly from the depth of the stage, with* Veturia *the mother of* Coriolanus, *and* Volumnia *his wife at their head, all clad in habits of mourning.* Coriolanus *stands at the head of the* Volsci, *surrounded by his lictors; but, when he perceives his mother and wife, after some struggle, he advances, and goes hastily to embrace them.*

CORIOLANUS *advancing.*

Lower your fasces, lictors ——
                    Oh *Veturia!*
Thou best of parents!

VETURIA.

Coriolanus, stop.
Whom am I to embrace? A son, or foe?

                              Say,

Say, in what light am I regarded here?
Thy mother, or thy captive?

CORIOLANUS.

Juftly, Madam,
You check my fondnefs, that, by nature hurry'd,
Forgot I was the general of the *Volfci*,
And you a deputy from hoftile *Rome*.

[*He goes back to his former ftation.*

I hear you with refpect. Speak your commiffion.

VETURIA.

Think not I come a deputy from *Rome*.
Rome, once rejected, fcorns a fecond fuit.
You have already heard whate'er the tongue
Of eloquence can plead, whate'er the wifdom
Of facred age, the dignity of fenates,
And virtue, can enforce. Behold me here,
Sent by the fhades of your immortal fathers,
Sent by the genius of the *Marcian* line,
Commiffion'd by my own maternal heart,
To try the foft, yet ftronger powers of Nature.
Thus authoriz'd, I afk, nay, claim a peace,
On equal, fair, and honourable terms,
To thee, to *Rome*, and to the *Volfcian* people.
Grant it, my fon! Thy mother begs it of thee,
Thy wife, the beft, the kindeft of her fex,
And thefe illuftrious matrons, who have footh'd
The gloomy hours thou haft been abfent from us.
We, by whate'er is great and good in nature,
By every duty, by the gods, conjure thee!

N 3
To

To grant us peace, and turn on other foes
Thy arms, where thou may'ft purchafe virtuous glory.

CORIOLANUS.

I fhould, *Veturia*, break thofe holy bonds
That hold the wide republic of mankind,
Society, together; I fhould grow,
A wretch, unworthy to be call'd thy fon;
I fhould, with my *Volumnia*'s fair efteem,
Forfeit her love; thefe matrons would defpife me—
Could I betray the *Volfcian* caufe, thus trufted,
Thus recommended to me—No, my mother,
You cannot fure, you cannot afk it of me!

VETURIA.

And does my fon fo little know me? me!
Who took fuch care to form his tender years,
Left to my conduct by his dying father?
Have I fo ill deferv'd that truft? alas!
Am I fo low in thy efteem, that thou
Should e'er imagine I could urge a part
Which in the leaft might ftain the *Marcian* honour?
No, let me perifh rather! perifh all!
Life has no charms compar'd with fpotlefs glory!
I only afk, thou would'ft forbid thy troops
To wafte our lands, and to affault yon city,
Till time be given for mild and righteous meafures.
Grant us but one year's truce: meanwhile thou may'ft
With honour and advantage to both nations,
Between us mediate a perpetual peace.

CORIO-

CORIOLANUS.

Alas! my mother! that were granting all.

VETURIA.

Canſt thou refuſe me ſuch a juſt petition,
The firſt requeſt thy mother ever made thee?
Canſt thou to her intreaties, prayers, and tears,
Prefer a ſavage, obſtinate revenge;
Have love and nature loſt all power within thee?

CORIOLANUS.

No,—in my heart they reign as ſtrong as ever.
Come, I conjure you, quit ungrateful *Rome*,
Come, and complete my happineſs at *Antium*,
You, and my dear *Volumnia*—There, *Veturia*,
There ſhall you ſee with what reſpeÐ the *Volſci*
Will treat the wife and mother of their general.

VETURIA.

Treat me thyſelf with more reſpeÐ, my ſon;
Nor dare to ſhock my ears with ſuch propoſals.
Shall I deſert my country, I who come
To plead her cauſe? Ah no! A grave in *Rome*
Would better pleaſe me, than a throne at *Antium*.
How haſt thou thus forſaken all my precepts?
How haſt thou thus forgot thy love to *Rome*?
O *Coriolanus*, when with hoſtile arms,
With fire and ſword, you enter'd on our borders,
Did not the foſtering air, that breathes around us,
Allay thy guilty fury, and inſtil
A certain native ſweetneſs thro' thy ſoul?
Did not your heart thus murmur to itſelf?

N 4　　　　" Theſe

" Thefe walls contain whatever can command
" Refpect from virtue, or is dear to nature,
" The monuments of piety and valour,
" The fculptur'd forms, the trophies of my fathers,
" My houfhold gods, my mother, wife and children!"

CORIOLANUS.

Ah! you feduce me with too tender views!—
Thefe walls contain the moft corrupt of men,
A bafe feditious herd; who trample order,
Diftinction, juftice, laws, beneath their feet,
Infolent foes to worth, the foes of virtue!

VETURIA.

Thou haft not thence a right to lift thy hand
Againft the whole community, which forms
Thy ever-facred country—That confifts
Not of coeval citizens alone:
It knows no bounds: it has a retrofpect
To ages paft; it looks on thofe to come;
And grafps of all the general worth and virtue.
Suppofe, my fon, that I to thee had been
A harfh obdurate parent, even unjuft:
How would the monftrous thought with horror ftrike
        thee,
Of plunging, from revenge, thy raging fteel
Into her breaft, who nurs'd thy infant years!—

CORIOLANUS.

Rome is no more! that *Rome* which nurs'd my youth;
That *Rome*, conducted by *Patrician* virtue,
She is no more! My fword fhall now chaftife
Thefe fons of pride and dirt! Her upftart tyrants!

Who

Who have debas'd the noblest state on earth
Into a sordid democratic faction.
Why will my mother join her cause to theirs?

VETURIA.

Forbid it, *Jove!* that I should e'er distinguish
My interest from the general cause of *Rome*;
Or live to see a foreign hostile arm
Reform th' abuses of our land of freedom.

[*Pausing.*

But 'tis in vain, I find, to reason more.
Is there no way to reach thy filial heart,
Once fam'd as much for piety as courage?
Oft hast thou justly triumph'd, *Coriolanus*;
Now yield one triumph to thy widow'd mother;
And send me back amidst the loud acclaims,
The grateful transports of deliver'd *Rome*,
The happiest far, the most renown'd of women!

CORIOLANUS.

Why, why, *Veturia*, wilt thou plead in vain?

TULLUS, *aside to* VOLUSIUS.

See, see, *Volusius*, how the strong emotions
Of powerful nature shake his inmost soul!
See how they tear him.—If he long resists them,
He is a god, or something worse than man.

VETURIA.

O *Marcius, Marcius!* canst thou treat me thus?
Canst thou complain of *Rome*'s ingratitude,
Yet be to me so cruelly ungrateful?
To me! who anxious rear'd thy youth to glory?

Whose

Whose only joy, these many years, has been,
To boast that *Coriolanus* was my son?
And dost thou then renounce me for thy mother?
Spurn me before these chiefs, before those soldiers,
That weep thy stubborn cruelty? Art thou
The hardest man to me in this assembly?
Look at me! Speak!

     [*Pausing, during which he appears in*
      great agitation. -

        Still! dost thou turn away?
Inexorable? silent?—Then, behold me,
Behold thy mother, at whose feet thou oft
Hast kneel'd with fondness, kneeling now at thine,
Wetting thy stern tribunal with her tears.

    CORIOLANUS.   [*Raises her.*

Veturia, rise. I cannot see thee thus.
It is a sight uncomely, to behold
My mother at my feet, and that to urge
A suit, relentless honour must refuse.

    VOLUMNIA.   [*Advancing.*

Since, *Coriolanus*, thou dost still retain,
In spite of all thy mother now has pleaded,
Thy dreadful purpose, ah! how much in vain
Were it for me to join my supplications!
The voice of thy *Volumnia*, once so pleasing;
How shall it hope to touch the husband's heart,
When proof against the tears of such a parent?
I dare not urge what to thy mother thou
So firmly hast deny'd——But I must weep——

            Must

Muſt weep, if not thy harſh ſeverity,
At leaſt thy ſituation. O permit me

               [Taking his hand.

To ſhed my guſhing tears upon thy hand!
To preſs it with the cordial lips of love!
And take my laſt farewel!

CORIOLANUS.

               Yet, yet, my ſoul,

Be firm, and perſevere——

VOLUMNIA.

       Ah *Coriolanus!*

Is then this hand, this hand to me devoted,
The pledge of nuptial love, that has ſo long
Protected, bleſs'd, and ſhelter'd us with kindneſs,
Now lifted up againſt us? Yet I love it,
And, with ſubmiſſive veneration, bow
Beneath th' affliction which it heaps upon us.
But O! what nobler tranſports would it give thee!
What joy beyond expreſſion! couldſt thou once
Surmount the furious ſtorm of fierce revenge,
And yield thee to the charms of love and mercy.
Oh make the glorious trial!

CORIOLANUS.

              Mother! wife!

Are all the powers of Nature leagu'd againſt me?
I cannot! will not!—Leave me, my *Volumnia!*

VOLUMNIA.

Well, I obey—How bitter thus to part!
Upon ſuch terms to part! perhaps for ever!——

                                  But

But tell me, ere I hence unroot my feet,
When to my lonely home I shall return,
What from their father, to our little slaves,
Unconscious of the shame to which you doom them,
What shall I say? ·

    [*Pausing: He highly agitated.*
Nay, tell me, *Coriolanus!*

CORIOLANUS.

Tell thee! What shall I tell thee? See these tears!
These tears will tell thee what exceeds the power
Of words to speak, whate'er the son, the husband,
And father, in one complicated pang,
Can feel—But leave me;—even in pity leave!
Cease, cease, to torture me, my dear *Volumnia!*
You only tear my heart; but cannot shake it;
For by th' immortal gods, the dread avengers
Of broken faith!——

  VOLUMNIA.   [*Kneeling.*
  Oh swear not, *Coriolanus!*
O vow not our destruction!

    VETURIA.
    Daughter, rise.
Let us no more before the *Volscian* people
Expose ourselves a spectacle of shame.
It is in vain we try to melt a breast,
That to the best affections Nature gives us,
Prefers the worst—Hear me, proud man! I have
A heart as stout as thine. I came not hither,
To be sent back rejected, baffled, sham'd,

       Hateful

Hateful to *Rome*, becaufe I am thy mother:
A *Roman* matron knows, in fuch extremes,
What part to take—And thus i came provided.

[Drawing from under her robe a dagger.
Go! barbarous fon! go! double parricide!
Rufh o'er my corfe to thy belov'd revenge!
Tread on the bleeding breaft of her, to whom
Thou ow'ft thy life!—Lo, thy firft victim!

CORIOLANUS.

Ha! *[Seizing her hand.*
What doft thou mean?

VETURIA.

To die, while *Rome* is free,
To feize the moment ere thou art her tyrant.

CORIOLANUS.

O ufe thy power more juftly! Set not thus
My treacherous heart in arms againft my reafon.
Here! here! thy dagger will be well employ'd;
Strike here! and reconcile my fighting duties.

VETURIA.

Off!—Set me free!—Think ft thou that grafp, which
binds
My feeble hand, can fetter too my will?
No, my proud fon! Thou canft not make me live,
If *Rome* muft fall!—No power on earth can do it!

CORIOLANUS.

Pity me, generous *Volfci!*—You are men—
Muft it then be?—Confufion!—Do I yield?
What is it? Is it weaknefs? Is it virtue?—
Well!—

VETURIA.

VETURIA.

What? Speak!

CORIOLANUS.

O, no!—my ftifled words refufe
A paffage to the throes that wring my heart.

VETURIA.

Nay, if thou yieldeft, yield like *Coriolanus*;
And what thou do'ft, do nobly!

CORIOLANUS. [*Quitting her hand.*
                There!—'Tis done!—
Thine is the triumph, Nature!
                [*To* VETURIA *in a low tone of voice.*
                Ah *Veturia!*
Rome by thy aid is fav'd—but thy fon loft.

VETURIA.

He never can be loft, who faves his country.

CORIOLANUS.   [*Turning to the* Roman *Ladies.*
Ye matrons, guardians of the *Roman* fafety,
You to the fenate may report this anfwer.
We grant the truce you afk.   But on thefe terms:
That *Rome*, mean-time fhall to a peace agree,
Fair, equal, juft, and fuch as may fecure
The fafety, rights, and honour of the *Volfci.*
                [*To the troops.*
Volfci, we raife the fiege.   Go, and prepare,
By the firft dawn, for your return to *Antium.*
                [*As the troops retire, and* Coriolanus *turns
                to the* Roman *Ladies;*
                TULLUS.   [*To* Volufius *afide.*
'Tis as we wifh'd, *Volufius*—To your ftation.
                            But

But mark me well—Till thou fhalt hear my call,
I charge thee not to ftir.   One offer more
My honour bids me make to this proud man,
Before we ftrike the blow—If he rejects it,
His blood be on his head.

VOLUSIUS.

Well! I obey you.

[*He goes out.*

CORIOLANUS.

Be it thy care, *Galefus*, that a fafeguard
Attend thefe noble matrons back to *Rome*.

SCENE II.

CORIOLANUS, TULLUS.

CORIOLANUS.

I plainly, *Tullus*, by your looks difcern
You difapprove my conduct.

TULLUS.

Caius Marcius,

I mean not to affail thee with the clamour
Of loud reproaches, and the war of words;
But, pride apart, and all that can pervert
The light of fteady reafon, here to make
A candid fair propofal.

6

CORIO-

CORIOLANUS.
Speak. I hear thee.
TULLUS.

I need not tell thee, that I have perform'd
My utmoſt promiſe. Thou haſt been protected;
Haſt had thy ampleſt, moſt ambitious wiſh:
Thy wounded pride is heal'd, thy dear revenge
Completely ſated; and, to crown thy fortune,
At the ſame time, thy peace with *Rome* reſtor'd.
Thou art no more a *Volſcian*, but a *Roman*.
Return, return; thy duty calls upon thee,
Still to protect the city thou haſt ſav'd :
It ſtill may be in danger from our arms.

CORIOLANUS.

Inſolent man. Is this thy fair propoſal ?

TULLUS.

Be patient—Hear me ſpeak—I have already
From *Rome* protected thee ; now from the *Volſci*,
From their juſt vengeance, I will ſtill protect thee.
Retire. I will take care thou may'ſt with ſafety.

CORIOLANUS.

With ſafety'--Heav'ns!--And think'ſt thou, *Coriolanus*
Will ſtoop to thee for ſafety ? No! my ſafeguard
Is in myſelf, a boſom void of blame,
And the great gods, protectors of the juſt.—
O 'tis an act of cowardice and baſeneſs,
To ſeize the very time my hands were fetter'd,
By the ſtrong chain of former obligations,
The ſafe ſure moment to inſult me—Gods !

Were

Were I now free, as on that day I was,
When at *Corioli* I tam'd thy pride,
This had not been.

TULLUS.

   Thou fpeak'ft the truth : It had not.
O for that time again ! Propitious gods,
If you will blefs me, grant it !—Know, for that,
For that dear purpofe, I have now propos'd
Thou fhould'ft return. I pray thee, *Marcius*, do it !
And we fhall meet again on nobler terms.

CORIOLANUS.

When to the *Volfci* I have clear'd my faith,
Doubt not I fhall find means to meet thee nobly.
We then our generous quarrel may decide
In the bright front of fome embattled field,
And not in private brawls, like fierce barbarians.

. TULLUS.

Thou canft not hope acquittal from the *Volfci*.

CORIOLANUS.

I do :—Nay more, expect their approbation,
Their thanks ! I will obtain them fuch a peace
As thou durft never afk ; a perfect union
Of their whole nation with imperial *Rome*
In all her privileges, all her rights.
By the juft gods, I will ! What would'ft thou more?

TULLUS.

What would I more ! Proud *Roman*; This I would;
Fire the curs'd foreft where thefe *Roman* wolves
Haunt and infeft their nobler neighbours round them;
          Extirpate

Extirpate from the bosom of this land,
A false perfidious people, who, beneath
The mask of freedom, are a combination
Against the liberty of human-kind,
The genuine seed of outlaws and of robbers.

CORIOLANUS.

The seed of gods !—'Tis not for thee, vain boaster !
'Tis not for such as thou, so often spar'd
By her victorious sword, to talk of *Rome*,
But with respect and awful veneration.
Whate'er her blots, whate'er her giddy factions,
There is more virtue in one single year
Of *Roman* story, than your *Volscian* annals
Can boast thro' all your creeping dark duration !

TULLUS.

I thank thy rage.   This full displays the traitor.

CORIOLANUS.

Ha! traitor !

TULLUS.

Firft, to thy own country, traitor !
And traitor, now, to mine !

CORIOLANUS.

Ye heavenly Powers !
I shall break loose—My rage—But let us part—
Left my rash hand should do a hasty deed
My cooler thought forbids.

TULLUS.

Begone—Return—
To head the *Roman* troops.   I grant thee quittance
Full

Full and complete of all thofe obligations
Thou haft fo oft infultingly complain'd
Fetter'd thy hands. They now are free. I court
The worft thy fword can do; whilft thou from me
Haft nothing to expeft, but fure deftruction.
Quit then this hoftile camp. Once more I tell thee,
Thou art not here one fingle hour in fafety.

CORIOLANUS.

Think'ft thou to fright me hence?

TULLUS.

      Thou wilt not then?
Thou wilt not take the fafety which I offer?

CORIOLANUS.

Till I have clear'd my honour in your council,
And prov'd before them all, to thy confufion,
The falfhood of thy charge; as foon in battle
I would before thee fly, and howl for mercy,
As quit the ftation they have here affign'd me.

TULLUS.

Volufius! Hoa!

SCENE III.

To them VOLUSIUS, *and Confpirators, with their
fwords drawn.*

TULLUS.

Seize and fecure the traitor!

CORIO-

CORIOLANUS.

[Laying his hand upon his sword.

Who dares approach me, dies!

VOLUSIUS.

Die thou!

*[As Coriolanus draws his sword, Vo-
lusius and the Conspirators rush upon
and stab him. Tullus standing by
without having drawn his sword.*

CORIOLANUS.

[Endeavouring to free himself.

Off!—Villains!

[Falling.

O murdering slaves! Assassinating cowards! *[Dies.*

SCENE IV.

*[Upon the noise of the tumult, enter hastily to them
GALESUS, the other deputies of the Volscian
States, Officers, friends of Coriolanus, and
TITUS with a large band of soldiers.*

GALESUS.

[As he enters.

Are we a nation rul'd by laws, or fury?
How! whence this tumult?——   *[Pausing.*

Gods! what do I see?

The noble *Marcius* slain!

TULLUS.

TULLUS.

              You fee a traitor
Punifh'd as he deferv'd, the *Roman* yoke
That thrall'd us broken, and the *Volfci* free!

GALESUS.

Hear me, great *Jove!* Hear, all you injur'd Powers
Of friendfhip, hofpitality, and faith!
By that heroic blood, which from the ground
Reeking to you for vengeance cries, I fwear!
This impious breach of your eternal laws,
This daring outrage on the *Volfcian* honour,
Shall find in me a rigorous avenger!
On the fame earth, polluted by their crime,
I will not live with thefe unpunifh'd ruffians!

TULLUS.

This deed is mine: I claim it all!—Thefe men,
Thefe valiant men, were but my inftruments,
To punifh him who to our face betray'd us.
We fhall not fear to anfwer to the *Volfci*,
In a full council of the ftates at *Antium*,
The glorious charge of having ftabb'd their traitor!

GALESUS.

Titus, till then fecure them.

        [*Tullus and Confpirators are led off.*

      [Galefus, *ftanding over the body of* Coriolanus,
        after a fhort paufe, proceeds.

             Volfcian fathers,
And ye, brave foldiers, fee an awful fcene,
                  Demanding

Demanding ferious folemn meditation.
This man was once the glory of his age;
Difinterefted, juft, with every virtue
Of civil life adorn'd, in arms unequal'd.
His only blot was this; that, much provok'd,
He rais'd his vengeful arm againft his country.
And, lo! the righteous gods have now chaftis'd him,
Even by the hands of thofe for whom he fought.

Whatever private views and paffions plead,
No caufe can juftify fo black a deed:
Thefe, when the angry tempeft clouds the foul,
May darken reafon, and her courfe controul;
But when the profpect clears, her ftartled eye
Muft from the treacherous gulph with horror fly,
On whofe wild wave, by ftormy paffions toft,
So many haplefs wretches have been loft.
Then be this truth the ftar by which we fteer,
Above ourfelves *our* COUNTRY *fhould be dear.*

The End of the Fifth Act.

EPI-

EPILOGUE.

Spoken by Mrs. WOFFINGTON.

WELL! Gentlemen! and are you still so vain
To treat our sex with arrogant disdain;
And think, to you alone by partial Heaven,
Superior sense and sovereign power are given;
When in the story told to night, you find,
With what a boundless sway we rule the mind,
And, by a few soft words of ours, with ease,
Can turn the proudest hearts just where we please?
If an old mother had such powerful charms,
To stop a stubborn Roman's conquering arms,—
Soldiers and statesmen of these days, with you
What think you would a fair young mistress do?
If with my grave discourse, and wrinkled face,
I thus could bring a hero to disgrace,
How absolutely may I hope to reign,
Now I am turn'd to my own shape again!
However, I will use my empire well;
And, if I have a certain magic spell

Or

Or in my tongue, or wit, or shape, or eyes,
Which can subdue the strong, and fool the wise,
Be not alarm'd : I will not interfere
In state affairs, nor undertake to steer
The helm of government,—as we are told
These female politicians did of old :
Such dangerous heights I never wish'd to climb——
Thank Heaven I better can employ my time——
Ask you to what my power I shall apply ?
To make my subjects blest, is my reply.
My purposes are gracious all, and kind.
Some may be told—and some may be divin'd :
One, which at present I have most at heart,
To you without reserve I will impart :
It is my sovereign will,—Hear, and obey,—
That you with candour treat this Orphan Play.

The End of the FOURTH VOLUME.

www.ingramcontent.com/pod-product-compliance
Lightning Source LLC
Chambersburg PA
CBHW020852020726
47497CB00005B/1369